The Secret of the
STONE HOUSE

The Secret of the
STONE HOUSE

JUDITH SILVERTHORNE

COTEAU
BOOKS
FOR KIDS

FROM MANY
PEOPLES

CHAPTER ONE

Emily squirmed in her seat and pressed her face against the car window. Scorching sun penetrated the enclosed vehicle, leaving her clammy and uncomfortable. Swirls of dust rose behind them as they floated by the lush green countryside, down the gravel road to Grandmother Renfrew's farm.

The closer they got, the more impatient Emily became. She was anxious to try her secret plan, but she knew urging her mother to step on the gas wasn't going to help. They were about eight miles off the Number One highway that cut like a hay swath through the southern half of Saskatchewan. They still had several miles to go, south down the "Moffat Road" between Wolseley and Candiac, and then a couple of miles east.

Just ahead, Emily could see the fir trees that grew around the Moffat Cemetery, where many of her family members rested. She thought about her ninety-six-year-old grandmother, who had been buried there three months before – the last time Emily had been to the farm. During that time in early springtime, she had begun the strangest experience of her life.

After her grandmother's funeral, she'd gone to their special place, an outcropping of rocks in the pasture. She'd climbed a large dolomite boulder that stood over the prairie like a sentinel and had been amazed to discover another girl already on the top ledge. The girl spoke with a Scottish accent and wore an old-fashioned ankle-length dress. Emily had been even more amazed to find that the girl, Emma, was from pioneer times. Somehow, Emily had ended up in the past with her.

Emily had always known the rock held a special quality, but had never expected to experience anything so unusual. It seemed that she could travel back in time whenever she and Emma arrived on the rock at the same moment. She made several visits this way, getting to know Emma and learning about pioneer life, but it was hard to manage, because the time of day in Emma's world was never the same as in the present. The girls solved the problem when Emma gave Emily a special stone that she could leave at the rock. As Emily held the smooth black stone and touched the boulder at the same time, she automatically appeared in Emma's world – until the stone had gone missing, ending her trips to the past. But on the last day of her visit, she'd found the stone again. She'd left it in her room in the old farmhouse, thinking she would never visit the past again. Now, three months later, she was ready to go back.

As they drew closer to the neatly kept cemetery, Emily strained to see out the driver's-side window. Kate reduced her speed somewhat, as if trying to make a decision, but then resumed speed.

"Wait! Mom!" Emily said in surprise. "Aren't we going to stop?"

Startled, Kate swerved slightly then steadied the wheels in the loose gravel. "I hadn't intended on it."

"But we have to!" Emily protested. "It's important!"

Kate blew her straggly bangs out of her moistened face. "Okay, already."

She pressed her foot on the brake, coming to a halt on the roadside in a cloud of dust and grasshoppers. They gazed over at the cemetery, with its wrought-iron gate and page-wire fence, to the spot where her Grandmother Renfrew lay buried. The dark marble headstone was already in place, but from the road, they couldn't see the inscription. All the monuments faced east, away from them.

Emily sprang out of the car first. She bent to pick stems of white daisies and black-eyed Susans growing along the ditch. Clutching them, Emily headed across the road and opened the tall metal gate with a plaintive squeak. Her mother's feet crunched on the gravel behind her, loud in the stillness of the day.

Once inside the gate, Emily stopped in silent reflection. She always felt a sense of awe and peace here. Close to the entrance, a replica of the nearby stone church held a map that plotted the burial sites, and a wooden stand with a pen and a guest register. Emily had signed it several times over the years.

"Let's not waste too much time," Kate steered her away. "Aunt Liz is waiting for us."

"*Waste* time?" Emily felt a stab of hurt as she followed her mom.

"I didn't mean it quite that way," Kate said, but didn't stop until she reached their destination.

Emily sauntered along the trimmed path, gazing over the mowed lawns, the occasional lilac bush, and the rows of stately headstones. Walking over to a far corner where some particularly old gravestones stood, she thought about the special people buried there, especially one close to her heart.

Wild roses bloomed all around a small headstone that read: *Emma, Beloved Daughter of George and Margaret Elliott, 5 May 1887 - 27 September 1899.* Emily's chest tightened as she remembered her pioneer playmate, Emma. She'd later discovered that she would have known Emma as her great-aunt, if Emma hadn't died so young. Instead, she was a dear friend to Emily, as close to her as any friend she'd ever known. She had run with her across the prairie and explored the meadows. They had shared adventures and worked together.

Emily had even been instrumental in helping to

rescue Emma's family from a deadly flu epidemic, although she had not been able to save her friend from later complications. The twelve-year-old girl had died after a long bout of pneumonia. Emily had tried to get back to her in time, but that was when the stone had gone missing and she could do nothing to help.

"Hurry up, Emily," her mother's irritating voice erupted into her thoughts.

Emily sighed and joined her at Grandmother Renfrew's gravesite. She thought again of her grandmother's funeral. She could almost hear the bagpipes playing "Amazing Grace" across the rolling prairie hills just showing the first touches of spring green.

Solemnly, Emily knelt and placed the flowers on the bottom ledge of the headstone, their petals bright against the black granite. She thought of the many times she and Grandmother Renfrew had picked wildflowers together. She missed her every day.

For several moments, Emily stood beside her mom in quiet contemplation. When she stole a glance, she saw that her mother's face had softened. As Emily looked out at the prairies, she felt her hand on her shoulder. Then felt a quick squeeze.

"They did a nice job of the engraving," her mother said, stepping back and swiping at a few mosquitoes that hovered nearby.

Engraving! Was that all her mother could think

about? Emily rolled her eyes. Kate glanced away, sweeping unruly strands of hair from her face. Then she strode back towards the car, flapping her top to get a little breeze on her body. With one last look, Emily followed.

Several sweltering miles later, Emily cranked down her window as they slowed to make the turn from the grid road into the lane of her grandmother's house. Along the ditches, sweet clover, foxtails, and white-flowered yarrow grew amid wild rose bushes pushed tightly against barbed-wire fences. The fresh summer air held a fragrant scent. Emily breathed deeply and sighed with pleasure. Her thoughts turned to her grandmother again and the times they'd spent exploring the pastures and fields.

Aunt Liz's car was in the driveway when they pulled to a stop by the impressive two-storey stone house. Made of local unpolished fieldstone, it was a large square-shaped home with curved arches above each of the many windows. Emily had spent many happy hours there.

As Aunt Liz came out on the veranda to greet them, Emily alighted from the car first and ran up the wide wooden steps. Engulfed in her aunt's strong hug, Emily caught the delicate bouquet of her perfume. Her aunt's blonde hair was dyed to hide the grey flecks, and cut into a stylish new bob. She was dressed in matching blue-green Capri pants and top that accentuated the aquamarine colour of her eyes. Although she'd been working, she didn't look a bit dishevelled, except for a slight brush of dust on one cheek.

As Emily watched her mom embrace Aunt Liz, the contrast was evident between the two. Her mom's long dark hair, caught up in a careless ponytail, had strands falling loosely about her face, framing her dark, serious eyes. Her lightweight tan pantsuit was crinkled from the long drive, and she seemed anxious.

"Kate, Emily, I'm so glad you're here. I've been going over everything and I have a few questions for you," Aunt Liz said, pulling Emily close to her.

"Nothing hard, I hope," Kate said, straightening her clothes and juggling her laptop computer, briefcase, and purse. "I don't think I want to deal with anything diffi-cult right now."

"Hmm," Aunt Liz replied, leading them into the house. "This divorce business is taking its toll, isn't it?" She gave Kate a light-hearted squeeze on the shoulder. "How about a cup of coffee? I have some freshly made."

"At least that's not a hard decision to make!" Kate sighed, setting her laptop down on the kitchen table, and plunking herself onto one of the antique wooden chairs. Aunt Liz poured her a steaming mug of coffee. Kate took a sip, then set it down.

"Did you want some apple juice, Emily?" asked Aunt Liz.

"No thanks, I'm going for a walk instead," Emily

said, edging towards the outside door. She couldn't wait to visit the sentinel rock.

Her mom and Aunt Liz exchanged a cautious glance. She knew they were thinking of the springtime, when she'd tried to convince them that her time-travelling adventures linked to the rock were real. Although they hadn't believed her at first, thinking she was making up stories because of loneliness or depression at the loss of her grandmother, she'd thought that in the end they had finally understood. Maybe they were just nervous about her going back again. Or maybe they hadn't believed her, after all.

Quickly, Aunt Liz said, "I've been going through everything again to make sure we're not giving anything we want away, or keeping anything we shouldn't. You might want to take a look too."

"Nah, that's no fun!" Emily groaned. "I'd rather be outside in the fresh air." It was more than that, though. They had come to prepare for Grandmother Renfrew's things to be auctioned, and she didn't want to think about that right now.

"Plenty of time for walks, Emily," her mother said, briskly straightening the tablecloth. "How about we bring in our stuff and get settled, then we can come up with a plan, so we can take all the time we want for other things."

Emily groaned. Her mom could be such a damper at times! Spontaneity just didn't come naturally for her. Emily plodded back out to the car and loaded herself down with luggage and other stuff that she'd brought for their week-long stay. Her mom and Aunt Liz followed her out, and within a few minutes, they'd lugged everything into their rooms on the two upper floors.

While Kate and Aunt Liz returned to the kitchen for their coffee, Emily remained at the top of the house. The attic had been divided in two long ago. One part was used for storage, and the other was an intriguing bedroom that Emily had used since she'd been old enough to be up there on her own. For a long time, it had been her own special world, where she was free to think and dream.

A nightstand and lamp stood to the left of the bed, which was centred along the slanted outside wall, right next to a dormer window with a wide ledge. A stream of sunlight filtered through the open lace curtains and across the gaily coloured handmade quilt and the carved headboard. A maple rocking chair sat off to the side beneath the window, and near the doorway sat a matching antique pressback chair.

At the end of her comfortable double bed stood an old wooden trunk with leather straps, which her grandmother's family had brought with them from Scotland in the mid-1890s. It was rumoured that some ancestor in her family had made it from old kegs used for storing beer in a public house they had operated. The trunk had been lovingly sanded and varnished so many times that the finish still gleamed. A tin address label painted with the words "Broadview, Assa., N.W.T." was attached on the side. Broadview was one of the train stations when the railroad first came through the west, and before Saskatchewan became a province in 1905. The area where her gran lived had been known as the District of Assiniboia, part of the vast North-West Territories of Canada.

Emily plunked her belongings on the bed, headed to the window, and opened it to look at the countryside out past the farmyard – at the silvery-green grass of the pasture, and beyond, at the familiar outcropping of rugged grey rocks. Among them, the three-metre high dolomite boulder stood overlooking the valley beyond. She and her grandmother had often gone there on their walks and had picnics. It was as if the rock had called to them – two kindred spirits in happy accord with the prairies. Emily breathed deeply of the fresh air and the scent of sage from the pasture. She felt her grand-mother's presence around her.

However, the rock meant even more to her. It was the gateway that took her to a long-vanished world.

With trembling fingers, Emily probed the gap underneath the window ledge. Yes, her journal was still there. She pulled it out and set it on the nightstand. Reaching deeper into the wall space, her fingers touched a soft cloth pouch. She let out a deep sigh, then drew it out. She sat down on the edge of the bed, turned the hand-embroidered pouch over in her hands, and pulled at the leather thongs to open it.

Then she poured the dozen or so stones onto the bed. They had belonged to Emma, who had brought the collection with her as mementoes of her Scottish homeland when they'd immigrated to Canada. Emily scanned the assortment of pebbles. It was still there! The smooth black stone looked so ordinary, but it was her channel to the past! Did she dare touch it?

She listened for noises down below. Her mom and aunt were on the second floor, discussing something, but she couldn't catch the words. Maybe this wasn't the best of times to try an experiment. Either of them could come up to her room unexpectedly, and she didn't want to start off on the wrong foot within a few minutes of arriving. Neither of them had been happy in the spring when she kept disappearing without any believable explanations of where she'd gone. They'd have a fit if she vanished now. Knowing she had the stone again thrilled her. She hoped it would be possible to go back in time again, but she could be patient.

Emily didn't know why or how the stone had disappeared before, but she suspected Emma's younger brother Geordie of taking it without realizing its significance. They'd often noticed him trying to follow them secretly, and he may have seen the hiding place. After Emma's death, the oval black stone had mysteriously reappeared. Emily had discovered it quite by accident, along with the rest of the stones in Emma's embroidered bag, concealed in her own bedroom in the gap under the window ledge. She had no idea how they came to be there.

Emily hadn't tried to go back into the past when she'd found the stones again, because Emma was no longer there. She and her mother had left the farm right afterwards. Since then, though, she'd had time to think about everything, and she wanted to see how Emma's family was doing, and spend some time with the baby who would grow up to be Grandmother Renfrew. This was the only way she could be close to her again. Her dying had left a deep well of sadness inside Emily that never seemed to go away. It was compounded by the sadness she felt about her parents' recent seperation and filing for divorce, but she didn't even want to think about that right now.

She heard quick footsteps on the stairs approaching her room.

"Emily?" Kate called from the other side of the door, tapping lightly. "What are you doing?"

Emily flipped her jacket over the stones and stood up just as her mom opened the door.

"Uh, just checking everything out." Emily shrugged her shoulders in an attempt to appear relaxed, even though her heart was doing little flutters against her ribs. She pointed to her sports bag on the floor. "Unpacking."

"Let's have a quick bite to eat and make our plans

for the auction." Kate left the room without waiting for Emily to answer.

Emily sat back down on the bed, defeated. Her mom had added more activities to their agenda and ignored what Emily wanted to do. The pattern was all too familiar. Did her mom do this on purpose to irritate her? Did she even think about how she affected everyone around her? Oh well, there was just no point in getting upset over her mother's attitude. She seemed extra harried and upset these days, because of *The Divorce.*

The news about her parents divorcing hadn't been a huge surprise to Emily when she'd thought about it afterwards. They'd hardly spent any time together as a family; always one parent or the other seemed to be gone. But when her parents finally voiced it, the reality of it had been like a sharp blow to the stomach. Mostly, she'd tried to stay numb, going about her life mechanically, but every once in awhile she felt an ache that just wouldn't go away. That was another good reason to get away from her mother by going out to the rock. Would she never escape today?

Emily eyed the jacket with the stones underneath it and decided they were safe for now. Her mom and her aunt weren't likely to come into her room unless she was there. And maybe it was just as well her mother had interrupted her. Right now, she shouldn't take any chances touching the black stone. She had to think about the consequences for awhile and come up with a plan. Consequences? Plan? She was beginning to sound like her ultra-organized mother!

In the kitchen, her mom and Aunt Liz had whipped together a spread of ham and Swiss cheese sandwiches, raw veggies, fruit, and Aunt Liz's fresh-baked Saskatoon pie. Emily tucked into them, remembering that they hadn't stopped for lunch on their trip there.

"Gerald Ferguson will be over at one to start hauling all the farm equipment into a row between the barn and the bins. His brother is coming to help too," said Aunt Liz, looking over a sheet of paper with a list on it.

"Donald is back?" her mom sounded surprised. "When did that happen?"

"He got back a month or so ago." Aunt Liz took a sip of her coffee and picked up her pen again.

"How long is he here for?" Kate persisted.

"My, aren't we interested all of sudden?" Aunt Liz said.

Kate shifted uncomfortably in her chair. "It's just that he swore he'd never come back to the farm life."

Emily stopped crunching on a carrot and stared at her mother. What was up with her? Gerald Ferguson and his wife were their closest neighbours, and they had rented Grandmother Renfrew's farmland for the past five years. But Emily didn't remember ever hearing of Donald before. How did he fit in?

"Things change. People change." Aunt Liz peered at

her over the top of her reading glasses. "Do I detect a little twinge of nostalgia?"

"Nonsense," Kate protested, reaching for Aunt Liz's list. "I'm just curious, is all!"

"So what's the deal, Mom?" asked Emily, sensing a juicy story. "Was he an old boyfriend or something?"

"Or something," her mom snapped. "Anyway, it was a long time ago!"

Aunt Liz raised her eyebrows.

"Let's get back to business. We only have two days to get this organized," said Kate. She pushed aside her plate and stared at the list. "Who's coming to help lug out the boxes of junk and the furniture on the front veranda and in the sheds?" she asked.

"It's all there," Aunt Liz raised one eyebrow at Kate, then took the list back.

Emily caught the faraway look on her mom's face, before she turned to stare out the window. Boy, this Donald person sure rattled her. He'd be here soon with Gerald, so she could get a look at him then. Maybe he would take her mom's mind off things for a while. On the other hand, maybe it wasn't such a good idea to have him in the picture. After all, her parents might get back together, even though they'd denied that was ever possible.

"Gerald made the arrangements for us with some of the other neighbours for tomorrow morning. The auctioneers are coming then too, to provide some guidance on where to place things," Aunt Liz read down the list.

"Agnes Barkley and the ladies from the Moffat community will serve the coffee and provide the snacks. Proceeds will go to the Moffat Church ladies auxiliary."

Emily grimaced when she heard the name Agnes Barkley. She was a busybody neighbour with a double chin and eyes like a hawk. She'd caused trouble in the past for Emily, spying on her when she'd gone to be with Emma.

Aunt Liz read down the list, "We just have to make sure we have all the essentials: coffee, teabags, juice, sugar, milk, paper cups, plates, napkins, and stir sticks, and anything else we think we might need."

"I suppose the auctioneer has someone to look after the accounting, bidding, and money things?" Kate asked absentmindedly

"Earth to Kate," Aunt Liz snapped her fingers playfully. "That's why we hired auctioneers!"

Kate blushed and ran her fingers through her bangs, then attempted to tuck the stray wisps of hair into her ponytail. "Good, then I guess we could head into town in the morning and run our errands."

Aunt Liz stood up and began clearing the dishes from the table. "Yes, and I thought we could take one more look over everything right away."

Kate nodded, putting the food away. "Okay, let's get to it!"

"Wait a minute," Emily protested. "Do you really

need me? I want to go to the rock."

Aunt Liz and her mom exchanged wary glances again.

"You'll see it soon enough," Kate cut in, motioning her to do the dishes. "You have work that needs doing."

"Come on, kiddo." Aunt Liz took Emily's hand and led the way.

Kate followed behind, mumbling about making the trek back up the stairs again and not looking forward to doing all the bedrooms. Emily remembered the stone lying on her bed. As they reached the second floor, she managed to move in front of Aunt Liz, hoping she looked natural.

"Speaking of bedrooms," Aunt Liz said, as they reached the attic floor, "Is there anything you want to get rid of in yours?"

She reached for the doorknob of Emily's room.

Emily stepped in front of the door before her aunt could open it.

"No thanks!" She sure didn't want her mom or aunt snooping around inside.

Her mom groaned, and pushed past Aunt Liz. "You're already going to have enough to furnish a whole house with what your grandmother left you!"

Emily smiled. "That's the idea!"

"Surely there's something you can give up?" Kate started to open the door.

Emily caught sight of the jacket she'd thrown over

the bed. One corner was flipped up! She could see the edge of the embroidered pouch.

"Do you have to throw your clothes about?" Kate asked, about to open the door wider and step in. "We just got here!"

Suddenly Emily blocked her mom's way, feeling her knees give a slight tremble at her daring. She didn't want them to see the stones! Her mom's eyes were still on the discarded jacket; she probably itched to hang it up. Emily tugged the door closed. "I'll hang my clothes up later."

Kate dropped her hand from the knob in surprise. "We still need to examine the lot."

"No, we don't," Emily said firmly. "I want to take everything!"

"We don't have room! Besides," Kate stepped back as if to assess Emily, "in a few years you'll probably change your mind."

Emily shook her head. "All these things are part of our past. They belonged to our ancestors. How could you not want them?"

"She has a point," said Aunt Liz.

Kate looked from her sister to her daughter in annoyance, as if she wanted to ask why Liz always seemed to end up siding with Emily. For a moment, it seemed to Emily that her mother looked smaller, more vulnerable.

"We've no place to store them," she said.

"Don't worry," Aunt Liz said gently. "We can leave them here until Gerald wants to do something with the house, if he ever does."

"Well, all right then," Kate conceded. She turned instead to the storage attic next to Emily's bedroom.

Emily let out a silent sigh of relief. Two close calls already. She had to help them get through this work as quickly as possible, so she could get back to the stones. She'd been thinking about them for weeks, half expecting they wouldn't be there. But now she had them and she had to figure out what to do.

CHAPTER TWO

Emily slipped over to the other side of the attic where the gradually slanted walls rose to a peak, allowing just enough room for most adults to walk upright down the centre of the room. The framing and beams were visible, and the walls unfinished like a ship's hold. Dust motes could be seen when they pulled on the strings of the bare light bulbs that lit the long, narrow space. Emily sneezed as their movements stirred up the dust.

Walking single file, Emily and her mom followed Aunt Liz past neatly stacked boxes and trunks of old things they'd decided to keep, including some furniture. They went by antique side tables, dressers, a rocking chair, and knick-knack tables for Emily when she was an adult.

Although she wasn't the only grandchild, no one else wanted anything more. Some of her aunts and uncles had taken a few pieces of furniture that belonged to the family, but they really weren't that interested in the past. Mostly the leftovers were things Emily had claimed before her mom and aunt could sell them in the upcoming farm auction.

When they reached the west end of the attic, Aunt Liz stopped beside a tall piece of furniture covered with a dust sheet. She removed the cloth to reveal a carved maple desk. Emily ran her hands gently over the hand-polished surface, touching the carved roses and ivy on the front. The desk stood about thirty centimetres taller than her and had a curved front with several hand-carved drawers below the drop-leaf.

"It's so beautiful," Emily said. "I still can't believe Gran left it to me."

"It is a superb piece of work," Kate said.

Aunt Liz laughed. "I take it, then, that we're all in agreement that this piece stays."

"As if there was any question," said Emily firmly.

"Just like all the other things," Kate said in exasperation. "Surely you don't need two rocking chairs!"

"Maybe I don't, but I think it would be best to decide that later when I do have my own home," Emily pointed out, feeling way older than her age.

Aunt Liz stared at the maple drop-leaf desk. "I seem to recall there is a hidden drawer in this desk somewhere."

She flipped the leaf down and began examining the tiny drawers and shelves.

"I don't remember anything like that," Kate said. "Come to think of it, I don't think I ever saw this desk downstairs."

"No, it was brought up here after our granddad passed away," Aunt Liz said. "Dad had his own desk and there was too much furniture cluttering the downstairs."

"I'm sure Mom didn't want to dust it, either," said Kate.

Emily was sure this true; her gran preferred being outdoors to doing housework. That's why Emily managed to spend so much time with her learning about their natural environment.

"Granddad loved hiding secret drawers and compartments everywhere," said Aunt Liz. "I only saw the inside of the desk once, when I was really small, and that was by mistake," she confessed. "Granddad didn't know I was in the room when he opened it and stuck in some papers. I'm sure he had the writing lid down and did something inside the desk to make it open."

Emily began to help Aunt Liz search, while Kate made suggestions about where to look. They poked and prodded, pulled out drawers, and felt inside all the cubbyholes. Some were deeper than others. Finally, Emily got down on her knees and pulled out all the drawers, handing them to her mom and Aunt Liz. As she peered into the shelves, she saw something metallic.

"There's some sort of hinge in there, so there has to be a door of some kind." She reached inside and began pushing on all the solid surfaces.

"I know Granddad didn't take all the drawers out," said Aunt Liz. "It's got to be simpler than that."

"Let's put them back in, then," said Emily. "I'll watch to see what happens to the hinge."

One by one, they placed the drawers back into position, starting with the bottom one first, until they'd replaced them all, but nothing changed. Emily examined the depth of the drawers, while Kate measured the exterior of the desk.

"There has to be something inside there," Kate guessed. "There's too much space left between the cubbyhole section and the back of the desk."

"Maybe it has something to do with the balance," Emily surmised. Slowly she pulled the bottom drawer out. When it was about halfway out, she heard a small *click*. She pulled a little more, but knew she'd gone too far. Pushing the drawer back into the "click" position, she tugged on the next drawer up, until it too clicked.

Behind her, Aunt Liz and Kate watched as she pulled out each drawer into its snicked position until she'd reached the top and had created a staircase effect. Still nothing happened. Remembering the placement of the hinge, Emily tugged on the front of the drawer section. All at once, the top segment swung open.

Emily gasped. "We did it!"

Secreted behind the top drawer section was a small compartment about ten centimetres high. Inside there was a sheaf of papers and a small envelope. Carefully,

Emily drew them out and handed them to Aunt Liz. She and her mom inspected the stack.

"The original homestead papers!" Kate said, examining them.

Aunt Liz and Emily moved in for a closer look at the legal-sized sheets. The old-style handwriting on the yellowed pages was difficult to read, but Emily managed to decipher some of it. Besides her great-grandfather's name, as the applicant for entry, she found his age, the quarter section of land he was applying for, mention of his wife, and the number of children.

Kate unfolded the next set of papers and found the patent application for the land, dated only a few years later. "He sure worked hard and fast," she said, noticing the dates of each document. "Sometimes it took people ten years or more to prove their homesteads."

"What does proving mean?" Emily asked.

Aunt Liz answered. "The homesteaders made an application of entry for a homestead, paying the ten-dollar registration fee, and then they had to "prove" it before they could apply for the patent. If I remember correctly, the proving part was living on the land for at least six months out of each year for three years, and making improvements, such as breaking a certain amount of land and constructing buildings."

"See here," said Kate, pointing to the homestead patent papers. "This describes all the improvements your great-grandfather made. He broke ten acres in 1899, thirty-five in 1900, and eighteen in 1901. He added twenty-seven acres in 1902, but then nothing in 1903, which seems odd."

"I bet that's because they built the stone house that year and didn't have time to do anything," Aunt Liz guessed. "Besides, they'd already met their requirements by then."

"Wow, there's even the size of buildings like the house, the barn, and the shed," Emily noted. "Look at how much they were worth! Eighty dollars for the house, and fifty dollars for the barn. And look at how much fencing he did!"

"Well, he had four strapping young sons to help him," Aunt Liz reminded them. "Still, it's impressive."

"Can I keep these for a while?" Emily asked, hoping to study them more.

"Sure," Aunt Liz said, folding them back up again.

"Handle them carefully, though," said her mom. "They're fragile."

"*Mom*," Emily said in an annoyed tone. Her mom must think she didn't have any sense at all.

Aunt Liz turned to the envelope. As she opened it, a small key fell to the floor. She picked it up and examined it.

"Look. It has a little tag attached with the letter *E* on it." She looked at Emily in surprise. "It must be for you." She handed it to her.

"I suppose," said her mom, reluctantly. "You are so much like your gran! Both pack rats!"

Emily wasn't sure if her mom was smiling or grimacing. Either way, Emily was glad she was going to be able to keep the furniture.

As they moved on to the boxes, Aunt Liz didn't even bother opening them. They were stacked and clearly labelled: a selection of pioneer clothing, glass negatives, photo albums, and the old camera and developing equipment her Grandmother Renfrew had used. As they scanned them, it was plain that everything was staying.

"Whew, that was probably the easiest floor to do," said Aunt Liz. "I thought it would be the worst."

"I guess we did a thorough enough job sorting in the spring," Kate agreed, heading back down the stairs. "Just seems like we didn't get rid of enough."

"We hauled plenty out," Emily said, remembering how many trips she'd made up and down the stairs, and out to the bins and veranda where everything was stored for the upcoming auction. Her mother seemed to guess what she was thinking.

"I'm not letting you anywhere near them," Kate said, looking pointedly at Emily.

Aunt Liz laughed, "Yeah, we sure don't want stuff coming back in!"

When they reached the second floor, they automatically headed into Gran Renfrew's old bedroom. The only furniture left in it was the oak bed, a matching dresser, and a little table with a lamp on it, for when they came to stay. A small stack of boxes with extra bedding and linens stood in one corner. Aunt Liz was using the room this time. Her mom had a smaller one down the hall, and the third one was already empty.

"You don't need me anymore, do you?" asked Emily, hopeful that she could escape. She fingered the key in her pocket and thought again about the stones lying on her bed. "You already know what I want, and I haven't changed my mind about anything."

Her mom sighed. "I suppose you can go for awhile. Just don't be gone too long," she cautioned. "I don't want to have to come looking for you."

Emily was already halfway up the stairs, dashing to her room to collect her stones. Now she could try out her plan! Excitement tingled throughout her body. She was free for a while at least.

She strode over to her nightstand with the key in her hands. She fingered it one more time, looked over at her bed and back at the key. Reaching a decision, she placed the key safely in the top drawer. She'd search for the box later. She didn't want to miss this opportunity to leave the house.

Closing her bedroom door securely, she listened for a few moments to make sure her mom and Aunt Liz hadn't decided to come upstairs again. As an extra precaution against any intrusions, she pushed the chair in front of the door and wedged it under the handle. Quickly, she changed from a pair of shorts into a pair of jeans. If she was successful returning to the past, she didn't want to shock anyone from the olden days by revealing her bare legs.

She gently lifted her jacket from the bed and laid it on the trunk to reveal the scattered stones once again. She picked each one up, rubbed it and returned it into the embroidered bag, skirting the special black stone and saving it to the end. It was crucial to her success. At least, she hoped so.

When she'd used it before, she'd slipped back a hundred years. Her fingers trembled as she reached out to pick up the mysterious stone.

Did it have any power left? Would she be flipped into the past, or did she need to be at the sentinel rock for it to work? If she touched it right where it lay, she had no idea where she might end up. Did she dare touch the stone now?

Mulling it over, she concluded she'd never gone anywhere by just touching the stone. Taking a deep breath, she clutched it. Moments passed. She remained on her bed. Sighing in relief, she tucked the stone into the pocket of her jeans, returned the others in the bag, along with her journal, to their hiding place under the window ledge. Then she removed the chair barricading the door and left the room.

She dodged her mom and Aunt Liz on the second

floor, with a brisk, "See you later."

"Be back soon," her mom called out.

Emily could hear the pair of them shuffling the boxes in the second bedroom. She didn't plan to be gone long. She only wanted to see if the stone still worked, until she hatched the rest of her plans.

The sun was probably at its hottest, Emily thought as she hurried across the yard and scrambled under the barbed-wire fence into the pasture. Overhead, swallows dove towards the barn. A smudge of tiny flies buzzed about her as she strode across grasslands ripe with summer flowers and blooming sage. The sky was clear and the air stifling, with no sign of a breeze. Crows cawed through the air and jays swooped onto fence posts.

Emily stopped and closed her eyes. She let herself drift, breathing deeply. She could almost feel her grandmother beside her. As she continued walking, she followed the same path they had often travelled together picking herbs and berries. She passed poplar bluffs filled with wrens and larks trilling their pleasure in the day. At times, she followed the deer trail over the rough terrain, dodging boulders half-hidden in the tall, tangled grass.

Heading up the gradual incline, she came at last to the outcropping of rocks. The special rock that she and her grandmother had climbed when Emily was younger sat on the edge of a coulee, overlooking a long shallow valley that stretched as far as she could see.

When she reached the base of the large dolomite rock, she stopped and thought through everything carefully. Moving to the front of the rock, she gave one last look across the meadow towards Grandmother Renfrew's stone house. She looked again at the patchwork of neatly fenced fields and pastures below, and then at the skyline to the tops of the elevators that marked the town of Glenavon, way off in the distance.

Circling the rock to the other side, with the makeshift toeholds scraped into the crevices, she stared across the flat prairie. Calmly, she pulled the stone out of her pocket and held it tight. Using her other hand, with palm facing outward, she closed her eyes and reached out to touch the rock.

CHAPTER THREE

The moment Emily touched the rock, her eyes popped open. *It worked!*

She couldn't stop grinning. In front of her was the familiar landscape of the past. Where flat open prairie had stretched in her own time, there was now a large bluff of aspen and scrubby brush. Wolf willow and silver sage dotted the wild countryside, broken only by a meandering creek. All the cultivated and fenced land had disappeared.

She'd done it! Now, could she get back home again? Successfully coming one direction didn't mean she could safely return. The way it had worked in the springtime was that she'd kept the stone in her pocket while she stayed in the past. When she wanted to return to her own time, all she'd had to do was leave the stone in a crevice of the sentinel rock. Would it all work the same this time? The only thing she could do was try it.

Cautiously, she slid the warm stone into the side pocket of her blue jeans. With trembling fingers, she let it go. Nothing happened. She sighed with relief.

Glancing over her shoulder at the stand of aspens, she looked for the trail she knew led to the Elliott homestead. From where she stood, she couldn't see it. I'll just take a quick peek she thought, reminding herself again that she needed to be home soon. Walking over to the aspen stand, she trekked around the outside edge, looking for the entrance to the trail. Where was it?

Sudden fear prickled the back of her neck. What if she hadn't come back to the right time period? She backed away towards the rock, looking for identifiable landmarks. The meadow to her left should be brimming with chamomile and medicinal plants, but everything was tall grasses and foxtails. The thicket of aspens seemed familiar, but something was different. All at once, she knew what it was. Everything had matured. The trees were bigger now and the grass meadows fuller and wilder.

Searching diligently and bending low, Emily at last found a narrow animal path through the trees. The family mustn't use it anymore. Everything had grown over. She fought her way inside the bluff, pushing branches out of the way and stumbling over the tangled undergrowth. Was she going in the right direction? She looked behind her and decided she could always find her way out again. She'd left a definite trail of broken twigs and trampled underbrush that anyone could follow. So much for her grandmother's teachings of leaving nature as she'd found it!

The air was humid and sticky as she struggled her way through to the other side of the dense trees. The season seemed to be similar to what she'd left behind, although she sensed it might be a little later towards fall. The mosquitoes found her without effort, and so did the tiny blackflies. Sweaty, scratched, and frustrated, she at last emerged into a clearing, and stood with her mouth gaping open.

The original dwelling site was gone! The small meadow in the centre of the trees seemed to be the same. But where once there had been an open firepit, and a clothesline stretched between two large poplar trees, now there was nothing. The rough fence made of branches to confine the pigs and the oxen had fallen down in ruins. She could see only traces of it. The spot where the three grey tents had been before the family had moved to their sod house was no longer visible. Quick-growing poplars encroached into the entire area. It was obvious no one had been there in a long time.

Emily's mind whirred with questions. Was she in the right time period? And if so, was this the right place? She retraced her steps in her mind. Yes, she'd definitely come in the right direction from the rock. But if the bluff of trees had grown to such a great extent, then how much time had passed?

She swung around, trying to get her bearings. Where was the Elliott family? Why couldn't she hear anyone working? Where was the well, and what about the path through the meadow that led to their sod house? Their home should be just across the small meadow and over the next rise, easily within hearing distance. Obviously, they no longer used this area for any of their needs.

Emily stumbled through the meadow in the general direction of the sod house. Oblivious to the tall grasses and thistles whipping at her legs and arms, she hurried to the top of the incline. She had only a few precious moments before she had to return home.

She reached the crest of the hill. There it was – the sod house. Only it was bigger now, and the yard was more developed. A lean-to had been added to one wall of the soddie, and some straggly delphiniums and lilies planted on either side of the doorway. But the place seemed deserted. There was no movement anywhere.

Except for the slight breeze that swished through the tall grass at her feet, the only sounds were distant calls of birds and the occasional *bzzt* of flies. Emily looked at the low angle of the sun. Why wouldn't someone be around at this time of the day? But there was no time to explore further.

Emily turned on her heels and headed back to the rock. Instinctively, she knew she'd been gone too long. She'd have to figure out the circumstances of the pioneer family on another trip. At least she was in the right place, although she wasn't sure what year it was. She'd always had trouble judging how much time must have passed in the present while she'd been in the past.

Running headlong across the final meadow, she jumped in fright and twisted an ankle when a sharp-tailed grouse rose in the tall grass in front of her. Shaken, she rubbed the ankle till it stopped hurting, then continued at a more careful pace, making as much noise as possible as a warning to other meadow inhabitants.

At last, she reached the special rock. Her chest heaved as she caught her breath and wiped the sweat from her face. She fished the stone from her pocket and stared at it. Obviously, she was going to have to leave the stone behind, if she wanted to return home. She didn't know whether she'd be able to find it again in the present, but there was no choice. She swept particles of dirt out of a deep crevice in the boulder about chest high.

She plopped in the stone with closed eyes, drew her fingers away, and squinted at her surroundings. She could see her grandmother's house a quarter of a mile away. She was in present time again!

But was that it? Were her adventures over? Or would she be able to go back to the past another time? Emily searched the crevice uneasily, and then exhaled with relief. She saw the stone. Looking around her to be sure she was home, she touched the rock with one hand and snatched the stone up again with the other. Instantly, she was back in the past, with its tangled grass, wolf willow, and sage.

Wahoo! She laughed aloud. She could travel at will now. Popping the stone back into its resting place, she found herself in the present. She breathed deeply of the sage and looked out across the fenced fields and pastures. Then she sprinted across the meadow for home, heat from the afternoon sun pounding down on her.

A dark green Ford pickup truck sped down the access road towards her grandmother's farmyard. It must be Gerald Ferguson and his brother Donald. She was panting now, and she wished she'd brought along a bottle of water.

At last, she reached the barbed-wire fence and crawled through it. The Fergusons hadn't yet arrived. She plodded up the porch steps, tuckered out.

Joining her mom and aunt in the kitchen, she headed straight for the cold water in the fridge. She gulped back a glassful, followed by a second one. She plopped on the edge of a chair to catch her breath.

"The Fergusons are on their way," she gasped out.

Instantly, Kate jumped up from the table where she'd been sipping coffee and working at her laptop. She began tidying up her papers and packing up her machine.

Aunt Liz watched with interest.

"I'm just clearing the table in case we need to use it," Kate said.

"Okay, if you say so," Aunt Liz teased.

Kate gave her sister a piercing look, as she left the

room with her arms laden. Moments later, the Ferguson's truck pulled into the driveway.

Emily joined Aunt Liz on the back porch as Gerald and Donald alighted from their vehicle. Donald was almost the spitting image of Gerald, except he was a tad shorter and wore his sandy-coloured hair longer around his ears. Both men reminded Emily of the common expression "beanpoles." They were thin and tall with long legs like a pair of stilts.

"Good afternoon, Liz," Gerald said in his reserved way, reaching out to shake her hand.

"Nice to see you again, Gerald," Aunt Liz smiled at him, "and you too, Donald."

But as she turned to shake his hand, he grabbed her up in a bear hug.

"It's been such a long time," he grinned as he released her.

"Indeed," she said with a wide grin.

Uh-huh, Emily thought to herself, Mom isn't the only one who finds him attractive.

"And you must be Emily," Donald advanced on her and took her hand firmly.

"Pleased to meet you, Mr. Ferguson," she said, noticing the crinkly laugh-lines around his warm blue eyes.

"Call me Donald," he said, laughing, "Otherwise I won't know who you're talking to."

"Okay," Emily agreed, liking him already. She pulled herself away and acknowledged his younger brother.

"Hello," she greeted Gerald.

He calmly shook her hand. "Nice to see you again, Emily."

Emily noticed how rough and callused his hands felt compared to his brother's. The screen door squeaked and her mother appeared beside her. She had tidied her hair and put on fresh lipstick.

"Hello, Gerald." She nodded a greeting, staring directly at him. Then she took a quick breath and turned to Donald.

"You've come home," she said with a slight smile.

"Just couldn't stay away," he grinned at her, then pulled her to him for a quick hug.

Flustered, Kate stepped back. "Do you want to come in, or shall we just get to it?" she asked.

"Still the same direct Kate." He laughed, leaning casually against a column on the porch.

"What about you? I'm surprised you're back at the farm," Kate retorted.

"People change, I guess," he answered with a relaxed shrug.

Her mom and Donald didn't seem to have anything else to say. They just kept looking at one another.

Aunt Liz interrupted the silence, "How about I get the keys, and we'll get started?"

"That would be fine," Gerald answered. "I'll go over and take a look at what needs to be done."

"Emily, I left the list on the kitchen counter. Will you get it for me while I grab the keys?" Aunt Liz signalled her to follow, leaving Kate and Donald on their own.

Inside the house, Emily asked, "Are you sure that was such a good idea, Aunt Liz?" She handed her aunt the list.

Her aunt grinned. "Not to worry. I'm sure your mom doesn't like it either, but they need to have a little time alone to get over their awkwardness. Might as well be right now."

Aunt Liz grabbed a huge ring of keys from a drawer and headed back outside. Taking an apple from the fruit bowl on the table, Emily crunched on it as she stared out the window. She watched Kate and Aunt Liz cross the yard with Donald to join Gerald at the barn. Aunt Liz handed the keys to Gerald and they stood for a few moments discussing arrangements about the farm equipment.

The two men began to sort through the keys, matching them to the machinery. Judging by their body language, Kate seemed to be trying to take over the key ring, but Donald snatched it up and dangled the keys just out of her reach. Donald seemed to be teasing her about it. Everyone laughed, even Kate. Emily took one last bite of apple and headed back outside. She wanted to know more about Donald. Anyone who could make her mom laugh was someone worth knowing.

Once they started moving the equipment, Emily grew bored. Besides, now that she knew how to get back to the past, she wanted to find out more about the Elliotts' lifestyle and new home. Over the roar of the machinery clanging and grinding into place, she signalled to her mom with her fingers walking across her palms that she was heading off again. She couldn't hear her mom's response, but there was no mistaking that she wanted her back soon. Emily held up two fingers and her mom nodded in agreement. Emily wasn't sure if Kate thought she'd be back at two o'clock or in two hours, but she wasn't waiting around to clarify it.

CHAPTER FOUR

This time Emily went more prepared. She changed into some lightweight sweatpants and a loose-fitting, long-sleeved shirt. Then she doused herself with bug spray and took some bottled water before she retraced her steps back across the pasture. When she reached the rock and transported back in time, she took the identical path to the homestead site. She found everything the same, although it seemed later in the day. She went over to the house and peered into the tiny windows. Obviously, no one was home.

Next, she tried the sod barn partially built into the side of a hill, but there wasn't even an animal inside. A pitchfork with broken tines leaned against one wall, but that was the only sign of habitation. The neatly stacked woodpile next to the barn seemed ready for use, and the yard was mowed, so obviously someone still lived here.

Emily circled the yard, poking into a little shed and what looked like a chicken coop before noticing a little outhouse tucked back into the trees. She came across rain barrels, and what she was sure was the entrance to the root cellar. Why didn't they have any animals about? Even if the oxen or cows were out to pasture, surely they'd have pigs and chickens? Stumped, Emily sat down on a makeshift bench beside the house, letting a warm breeze waft over her perspiring face.

She tried to recall which direction the garden was from the house, but changes in vegetation disoriented her. She thought about possible reasons everyone would be gone. Maybe they'd all gone to town, but it didn't seem logical for ten people to go at once, unless some were working in the fields or garden while the others had gone. But if some of them were about, why couldn't she hear them?

She strained to make out any kind of sounds beyond the rustling of the poplar leaves and the twittering of birds. She would have expected to hear the ring of axes, or the clanking of the harness as the oxen worked the land. So where had everyone gone? Then she noticed a well-worn trail behind the barn. Maybe she'd follow it to see where it led. If she could find the garden and the cultivated fields, she'd know for sure someone still lived here.

The trail wound through scrubby brush and over a small rise. Emily had just started down the incline when she was startled by sharp barking. In the distance, she could make out the form of a dog bounding in her direction, and moments later, a human shape became clear. As the shapes drew closer, she saw a tall boy with a border collie well in the lead.

"Hello," he called out long before he reached her.

At least he's friendly, Emily thought, still not sure about the dog. But the collie rushed up to her, sniffing at her, then licking at her hand, as if expecting to be petted. She gave the dog a scratch behind the ears.

"You're sure friendly," she said, giving it long strokes down its back patches of black, white, and gold. The collie wagged its tail happily.

Emily noticed the boy's jolt of red hair first. Then his cheerful face smattered with freckles. He looked so familiar. She gasped. At the same time, astonishment registered on the boy's face.

"Is that really you, Emily, lass?" he asked with a Scottish lilt to his voice.

"Geordie?" she guessed.

"Yes, it's me," he assured her. "I never expected to see you again. Where have you been hiding?"

"Not far away," she answered, still stunned. The last time she'd seen him, he'd been eight years old and much shorter. "You've grown so much," she said.

"Aye, that I have," he answered. "But then, I'm older too."

"How old?" she asked eagerly.

"Well, I would be twelve now, going on thirteen," he answered proudly. "Doesnae look like you've aged any, though to be sure, you look a mite shorter to me now."

"Four years have passed?" Emily could hardly take the information in. That meant it was 1903.

He nodded. "We lost Emma, you know."

"I know, I'm so sorry." Emily felt her throat constrict with grief. "I wish I could have helped her."

"Aye, lass," he said touching her arm. "There was naught you could do. Though I wondered why you never returned."

She wasn't sure how to answer. Perhaps she could have helped Emma, she didn't know. And how could she tell Geordie that he might have been the reason she couldn't get back to help? She looked out across the prairie, trying to let go of her sorrow. Overhead, a V of geese honked in the lowering sun.

Suddenly she exclaimed. "But you can see me!"

"I always could," he said, grinning. "Why do you think I followed you and Emma everywhere?"

"I knew that was you! Although you were pretty good at keeping hidden," Emily admitted. She'd thought only Emma could see her, although their granny had sensed her too.

"I was good, wasn't I?" he laughed, his face turning a little red.

"Too good," she added, not able to resist a little poke at him.

She thought again about the possibility that he had taken the smooth black stone from the crevice of sentinel rock, which stopped her from returning to visit them in the springtime. His mischief may have caused serious repercussions for Emma. But she didn't want Geordie to feel bad. Besides, there wasn't anything they could do about it.

"Where have you been?" Geordie asked, looking at her in a puzzled way.

"Woolgathering," she answered, bringing her thoughts back to the present.

"For sure," he said, "but I mean for the last four years. I never could figure out exactly where you came from." He shoved his hands into his overalls and waited for her to answer.

Whew! That was going to take some explaining!

"What do you know of the second sight?" she asked.

"I know my granny and Emma both had it," he answered. "They could tell things about people and about the future. Premonitions and such."

"Well, then you probably know they see things in visions...in their minds."

He seemed unsure of what she meant, eyeing her suspiciously.

"Or it could be like dreams. You have dreams, right?"

He nodded.

"Have you ever had a dream so real you actually thought it was taking place?"

"I suppose I have," he admitted.

"Well, what if you dreamt about the past, when you lived in Scotland, or if you dreamt about what it would be like to live in your grandparents' time?"

He thought about that for a few moments. "All right," he nodded, reluctantly.

"Well, that's kind of what it's like for me," she said. "It's like I'm dreaming about what happened in my past, only everything is very real to me."

"But how come you're real to me, too?" He stepped back, uneasily.

"I don't understand it myself," she said. "But maybe you're dreaming about the future and I'm dreaming about the past, but we're both in the same dream and able to talk to each other."

He thought about it for a few moments. "I think I understand better now," he said, although he still kept his distance from her.

"Good. I know it's hard to believe," she said. "I can't really explain how it happens, but I know Emma understood too."

He smiled. "Yes, you were a special friend to her."

Emily sighed, as she pictured Emma when she first met her – her laughing face surrounded by blonde braids that hung halfway down her back. The two of them would sit atop the sentinel rock, with their hair gently wafted by the wind, Emma in her long dress and high-buttoned shoes swinging over the edge, and she in jeans with her sneakers.

Or they'd walk on the prairie, sharing each other's knowledge of plants or picking mushrooms after a rain.

"You helped save our lives, you know," Geordie interrupted her thoughts.

Emily knew he was referring to the time she and Emma struggled to save the Elliott family during a dangerous flu epidemic.

"Maybe a little," she said. They hadn't been very successful with Emma's granny, who had died.

As if reading her thoughts, Geordie said, "Granny was already dying. There wasn't anything anyone could do for her."

Emily closed her eyes and felt her throat tighten with emotion.

"You and Emma, you made a good pair." Geordie said. Then to change the subject, he said, "Do you remember when I pitched the salamander at you?"

Emily giggled. "Yeah, Emma was sure quick to chase you with it." They'd been sitting on a blanket braiding onions in the warm autumn sun, when Geordie had snuck up on them.

"That's why I always teased her," he admitted. "She never let me get away with anything."

"She certainly stood up for herself," Emily agreed, torn between wanting to hear more about Emma and wanting to push the sad memories away. The choice was made for her, though, because she knew she couldn't stay much longer.

"I need to go home," she said, "but tell me first, why is there no one at your house?"

"We are building a new one," he said, pointing back the way he'd come. "Everyone is helping so we can move in soon."

"But why are there no animals at your old place?"

"We've already moved them, so we can care for them during the day while we're working. Would you like to see our new place?" Geordie said eagerly.

Instantly, Emily became excited. But should she risk taking the time to go? "How far is it?"

"Just across the pasture," he motioned.

"Well, if we hurry," Emily came to a sudden decision. She'd chance going and hope her mother wasn't expecting her yet. She could always say she'd meant she would be gone for two hours, though she knew even that time was probably almost up.

"Come on, Sorcha," Geordie called.

They raced across the prairie with the border collie trotting ahead of them. Emily's heart pounded in her chest as she ran over the rough terrain. Excitement bubbled inside her too. At last, she was going to reconnect with Emma's family.

As they dropped over a rise, Emily stopped abruptly. Geordie almost ran into her. Sorcha barked at the sudden change of plan and returned to them, wagging her tail. Emily stared in astonishment. At the bottom length of the pasture stood a stone house – her grandmother's stone house.

CHAPTER FIVE

Emily stared at the partially built stone house, already almost two storeys high. Scaffolding surrounded the walls with plank ramps jutting to the ground below. Two of Geordie's older brothers shunted a huge fieldstone up the ramp and placed it on top of one wall. Two other men, one on the ground and the other at the top of the wall, hoisted pailfuls of mortar, using a system of ropes and pulleys. Someone else straddled the wall and trowelled the mortar in place.

A young woman came down a trail that led from a pit dug into a hillside, pushing a wheelbarrow towards the house. A fire burned briskly in the pit, and from the acrid smell, Emily knew it must be where the lime was being prepared. On the ground, two women struggled to lever a heavy granite rock onto a plank. Several piles of different-sized rocks dotted the ground behind them. Two young girls sifted gravel, catching the fine sand, which Emily assumed was for mixing with the lime to produce the mortar. She wasn't sure who all the people were from this distance, but she was positive Geordie's whole family must be there, including his mom and sisters. There also seemed to be an extra man helping.

"Isn't it grand?" Geordie asked at her elbow.

"It's beautiful," Emily whispered. How incredible to see her grandmother's house in the making!

"Bet you've never seen anything so splendid," he said.

Emily smiled at him. "Actually, I have," she said. "I'm staying in this very same house."

His eyes widened in surprise. "How could you? Oh..." Sudden realization seemed to strike him and he began to laugh. "Of course, you are from my future."

Joining in his laughter, Emily nodded. "Incredible, isn't it?"

"Indeed! Would you like a closer look?"

"I would," said Emily, "but I can't right now. I have to get back home."

"At least you're not far," he said chuckling.

"True," she answered, "but I can only go back and forth between your world and mine at the rock."

"I always wondered how you did it," Geordie waited for her to explain.

When she told him about the need for the smooth black stone and how she'd left it at the sentinel rock between times, a sudden stillness came over him.

"Show it to me."

She pulled it out of her pocket and opened her hand.

"Don't take it," she warned, "I don't know what will happen." A surge of fear raced up her spine.

Geordie stared at it intently. "It was because of me, wasn't it? Because I took the stone, you couldn't come back?"

Emily said nothing.

"I'm so sorry, lass." His voice cracked. "You might have saved Emma's life?"

Emily shook her head, coming to a sudden realization. "No, Geordie, I don't think I could have saved her. She was too sick. I don't think even the medicine in my world would have worked."

Emily knew what she said was true, although she'd wanted to blame someone, and Geordie in particular, for Emma's death. Seeing him in anguish in front of her now, she knew it hadn't been his fault.

"Let's just remember the good bits," Emily said softly, touching his arm. "Emma and I enjoyed our time together and I know you were close to her too."

He stared unhappily at his feet.

Quietly, she said, "I have to go now, but I'll come back again."

He nodded, unable to speak.

She left him then, turning back only once to see him stumbling towards the construction site. Replacing the stone in her pocket, she jogged back to sentinel rock, skirting the old homestead and the bluff of trees now that she had her bearings.

Her sadness lifted as she cut across the prairie, avoiding gopher holes, large protruding stones, and hummocks of grass. By the time she reached the big rock, she was smiling to herself. How ironic that that she was going to have to go back over the same ground she'd just covered in order to get home again. If only she could think of a way to get back and forth in time right at the stone house. She'd sure save a lot of time and energy!

When Emily returned to the yard, she saw the machinery lined up in the typical auction format of small implements to large ones, with the more expensive ones, like the tractor, grain truck, and combine at the end of the row for sale at the very last. Otherwise, the yard was deserted. She found everyone in the kitchen having coffee. Her mother seemed to be in command, as usual.

"Where have you been, young lady?" she demanded, pointing to the clock that ticked at a quarter past three. "I thought you said you'd be back by two?"

"No, in two hours," Emily said, ready for the challenge. "I'm right on time!"

Her mother raised her eyebrows in surprise. She knew when she'd been outsmarted.

"What makes the pasture so fascinating?" Donald asked, reaching for another scone and slathering it with butter and wild raspberry jam.

Emily slid into a chair and reached for a glass of milk.

"There are all kind of neat things up there," she answered. "Gran and I used to go together all the time. We used to pick plants and flowers. I was just checking out all our old haunts."

"I seem to recall there's a spectacular view from that huge old rock on the edge of the coulee," he said. "I suppose you can still see the grain elevators at Glenavon?"

"Not for long, I'm sure," said Gerald. "They're tearing them down next month."

"It's such a pity to see these old landmarks disappear," Donald remarked.

"I didn't know you cared. Last I heard, you'd had enough of rural life," Kate said, surprised. "I thought you didn't find it fulfilling enough."

"I can still appreciate important traditions and landmarks," Donald replied. "Guess I've mellowed a little over the years."

Emily observed the interchange, noticing her mom and Donald eyeing each other.

"So what's left to do for the auction?" She peered at everyone sitting around the table.

"Just the small stuff," said Aunt Liz, reaching for the auctioneer's instruction sheet.

"I assume everything is already sorted into boxes?" Donald gave Kate a light smile.

"All ready to go," she grinned back at him.

"Well then, seeing as how Kate is so on top of things," Donald said, "maybe we could make sure some of the other gear like the air compressors, rototillers, posthole augers, and such are in place right now."

Donald caught Gerald's eye.

"Sure." Gerald nodded.

Donald took a long sip of his coffee, staring intently at Kate over the rim of his cup until she blushed. Then he pushed back his chair.

Innocently, Emily got up and headed for the door behind the men. "I think I'll get a little fresh air. It seems a little hot in here."

Aunt Liz chuckled behind her. Kate clattered the dirty cups and plates as she gathered them. Emily didn't know what to think. She liked Donald, but wasn't sure about the effect he was having on her mom. She didn't like the thought of anyone replacing her dad in her mom's life.

Emily hung out on the porch watching the two men head over to the Quonset. There was nothing of interest for her there; chainsaws, welding gear, ladders, and table saws were the last thing she wanted to look at. On the other hand, it might be worth taking a closer look at her grandparents' stone house. She'd always taken it for granted before, never considered how or when it was built.

She walked into the middle of the yard and stared up at the north side. She wondered how long it would take to build. She'd have to ask Geordie the next time she saw him. She started counting the stones on one wall as Aunt Liz emerged.

"Whatever are you doing?" She tried to follow Emily's gaze.

"I just wondered how many rocks it took to build this house."

"Plenty," Aunt Liz said. "Do you know who built it?"

"I thought it was my great-grandfather and his family," Emily answered, knowing she was right.

"Well yes, they did work on it, but they had help from a full-fledged stonemason, one of the best in the area, by the name of William Gibson. He built quite a few homes around here in the early 1900s."

Emily realized the extra person she'd seen helping the Elliotts must be Mr. Gibson. "It sure was a lot of work," she said. "Especially when they had to do everything by hand."

Aunt Liz looked at her oddly. "They didn't have any cement mixers, like that," she agreed, pointing to the one that Gerald was just rolling outside the Quonset. "I can't imagine how they did it all."

"By ramps, pails, and using ropes," Emily said. Immediately, she realized her mistake. She shouldn't have any first-hand knowledge.

"How do you know that?" Aunt Liz quizzed her.

"I'd say she's just a smart young lady," Donald said coming up behind them. He stared at the house. "The workmanship on these places has always impressed me. Tons of stone went into them. Literally."

"Especially when you consider these walls are twenty-four inches thick," said Gerald, joining them. "Some were only eighteen inches."

"The men would have been in great physical shape when they were done," Aunt Liz laughed.

And the women too, Emily thought.

"You're not kidding," Donald agreed. "Did you know stone weighs one hundred and fifty pounds per square foot, and it takes seventy-two tons to build a six-hundred-square-foot house? And this one's almost three times as big." He grinned as everyone looked astounded. "I read that in a history of this area."

"And do you know what that translates into in metric?" Kate sidled up to them. She'd come outside and around the corner of the house without anyone noticing her. She held a calculator and notebook, where she'd written down Donald's numbers. After a rapid series of calculations, she announced, "That means there are almost 196,000 kilograms of stone in our house, and it is over one hundred and sixty-seven square metres, with walls that are sixty centimetres thick."

"Mom, go back to your office work," Emily suggested playfully.

"I'm on my way," she said, walking back into the house.

The others dispersed too; the Fergusons back to the Quonset and Aunt Liz with them to check on how they were doing. Emily suddenly remembered the key. Now was as good a time as any to do a little search. She passed her mom at work on the laptop at the kitchen table. Kate barely noticed her; she was concentrating hard on some financial figures on the screen.

When she reached her attic room, Emily sat on the edge of the bed and drew the key out of her nightstand drawer. She studied it, wondering what type of box it would fit and what might be inside. She suddenly wished she'd known her great-grandfather before he died. What kind of person was he? If only she knew how his mind worked, she might be able to figure out where he'd hidden the box.

They'd searched the desk so thoroughly looking for the hidden compartment, that she knew the box wasn't there. She'd never come across anything like it in her room, so that idea was out. The bedrooms on the second floor had been checked thoroughly and she'd been present when they'd packed the boxes in the attic and on the main floor. She didn't know where else to look. Emily sighed and set the key aside.

Pulling out her journal, she began jotting down her experiences since her arrival. She wrote until her hand cramped up, then lay back on her bed and thought about Geordie. He'd grown so much. She mustn't wait too long to go back – the time sped quickly by in the past. Everything was always a jumble with different seasons and different days in the two worlds. Was there some formula to it? If only she could figure out a method for calculating it, so she'd know in advance the time she'd be visiting. As she contemplated this dilemma, she felt herself drifting into sleep.

Sometime later, muted talking brought her back to consciousness. She couldn't make out the words, but they sounded important, judging by the tone of voice. Shaking off sleepiness, Emily looked over at her clock. 5:10 p.m. She swung her feet off the bed hitting the floor with a thud. Placing her journal in its hiding spot, and the key back in the drawer, she headed downstairs.

When she reached the second level, she heard her mom in her bedroom. Emily poked her head around the partially open door. Kate stared out the window with the phone receiver in her hand, her expression blank.

"Okay, David," she said with an exaggerated patience in her voice, as if placating an upset child. "Then I guess there's nothing more to say." She listened again. "Fine." She hung up with a slam.

"Mom?" Emily hesitated in the doorway.

Kate whirled around, startled.

"What did Dad say?" Emily tried to keep the anxiety out of her voice.

"Nothing good!" Kate scowled. She turned and looked out the window again.

A few moments later, she went over to Emily, her emotions in check. She gave her a hug. "Except that he misses you," she whispered into Emily's ear.

"Could I call him back?" Emily asked. Her mother hesitated before answering.

"Yes, but give him a few minutes to calm down. He's on one of his rants."

Great, thought Emily, he probably wouldn't even answer the phone, if he thought it was her mom calling him back. Obviously, the negotiations between her parents were not going well. That also meant her mom wasn't in any mood to consent to her going out again today, especially since it was so close to suppertime. She could already hear her aunt rattling around in the kitchen. She might as well go help.

Her stomach growled as she descended the stairs. The smell of roasting chicken wafted up to her. Aunt Liz was a good cook.

CHAPTER SIX

B y the time Emily left for the sentinel rock the next morning, the sun was just breaking over the horizon. Unable to sleep, she'd tiptoed out of the house before anyone else was up. Dew glistened on blades of grass and birds twittered their greetings to the day as she strolled across the meadow, spotted with patches of yellow buffalo bean and tiny blue harebells. Emily felt content and full of excitement. She hoped she would find Geordie alone so she could talk to him. But that might not be so easy with his large family around and all the work they had to do.

Once she'd transported herself into the past, Emily decided to go to the old homestead and follow the trail from there to the stone house. She dodged around the aspen stand, avoiding unnecessary steps. She wondered again if there was a way to come and go right at the new home place.

As she approached the sod home, Emily heard voices and the clang of an axe chopping wood. By the time she reached the yard, she found the place full of activity. She watched from behind a sturdy caragana bush, trying to place each of the Elliott family members.

George Senior, her great-grandfather, looked about the same, with his grey whiskers and hair, and his smiling eyes. He seemed to be mending some kind of frame with a screen in it. Geordie was hauling firewood to the house, while one of his older brothers split the wood and another stacked it. She was pretty sure they were Duncan and Jack. Another young man she thought was Sandy, the oldest, seemed to be removing hinges from the barn door.

Beth and Kate must be the two younger sisters, folding sheets as they took them off the clothesline at the side of the house, laughing as they tried to shoo a grasshopper off the material. Bella, the oldest sister, didn't seem to be around. Perhaps she was doing chores inside the house.

Elsbeth, Geordie's mom, sat on the bench in front of the house, handstitching clothing. Beside her sat a little girl with brown pigtails, lining up several spools of different coloured thread for her mom.

"Good girl, Molly," said Geordie's mom.

Emily stared in amazement. *Molly.* Her grandmother. The last time she'd seen her, Molly was a baby. Now she looked four years old.

Emily edged her way into the yard, closer to the sod house, hoping no one could see her. As she advanced, Molly looked straight at her and smiled.

Emily stopped in her tracks. Oh, no, Molly was able to see her too.

Geordie's mom stared in the direction Molly was now heading, but appeared not to see anything.

"Where are you off to, lass?" she dropped her mending and looked about anxiously. "Molly, come here."

Emily held up her finger to her lips in a shushing gesture and winked at Molly. Molly giggled and tried to wink back. Her mom snatched her up and carried her into the house. Molly grinned over her shoulder and waved, as Emily stepped back into the shadows of the trees. So much for not attracting any attention. If only she could get Geordie to notice her without upsetting anyone else.

She waited until he brought the next load of firewood to the house, then stepped into the open.

"Geordie," she said softly.

Startled, he almost tipped the wheelbarrow. Then he grinned. He scanned the yard to see if anyone was watching, then parked the wheelbarrow by the door and pulled Emily around the corner of the soddy.

"Hello, lass. It's grand to see you," his eyes twinkled. "I wondered when you'd come again."

"Why aren't you working on the stone house?" she asked.

"It's Sunday," said Geordie as it that explained everything.

He noticed her puzzled gaze. "We don't do any heavy work on Sundays, except for the basic things that need doing here, so we can concentrate on building the rest of the week."

"I see," Emily said, disappointed. "I was hoping to see more about how you built with stone, but I guess I'll have to come back another time."

Geordie grinned. "You're in luck. It's my last load of firewood and then I need to go feed the chickens and pigs at the other site. So I can take you to look at the house without anyone being there."

"Wonderful!" Emily clasped her hands excitedly.

"This will be the first time I won't mind doing the women's work," he added. Again Geordie realized she didn't understand. "Usually my mum or the girls feed the critters, but I have to do it until we move. My dad is always giving me the minor chores to do." He shook his head and nodded at the others working in the yard. "My older brothers get to do all the important stuff."

Although he made light of it, Emily sensed he was bothered a great deal by not being given the work he considered men's work. She couldn't imagine what it must be like having three older brothers to compete with.

"I'm sure what you do is necessary too," she said lightly. Sometimes her mother also acted as though Emily couldn't handle important tasks.

"Aye, I guess it all needs to be done," he smiled, shaking off his glum thoughts.

Emily touched his shoulder. "I'll wait for you on the hill."

"See you there," Geordie agreed, going back to unload the firewood.

Emily strode towards the barn, confident that no one else could see her, although she wondered why. It seemed that only the younger children could, but that didn't explain why Beth and Kate couldn't detect her. They were younger than Geordie and older than Molly – about nine and eleven by now. Perhaps they didn't have any "knowing" at all, as her gran would have called it. This "second sight" came naturally to Emma, and obviously to Molly. There seemed little doubt that Geordie also had it, although he didn't seem to acknowledge it.

On the crest of the hill, Emily sat on a flat rock, staring out across the prairie with its abundant buckbrush and wolf willow. She could almost picture Emma coming to meet her. She remembered how they would lie on the ground, watching the clouds move across the sky, and have contests in naming the birds that flew overhead. And she remembered the fun they'd had figuring out their family connection.

Even now, Emily found herself amazed, knowing that the Elliotts were her relatives from the past. Should she tell Geordie? Wouldn't he be surprised to find out he was her great-uncle and that Molly was her grandmother? It was a rare gift seeing her gran as a small child. Molly had recognized Emily as a kindred spirit right from the beginning, when as a baby she had first smiled at her.

"What are you grinning about?" Geordie's voice startled her.

Emily jumped up, brushing the grass off her clothes. "Just at how pleased I am to be here," she said.

"I'm glad you're here too, lass," Geordie said as they walked around a patch of flowering chamomile.

"Tell me why you've decided to build the house so far from your other place," Emily asked.

"There's a better well over there," he said. "We're also going to have easier access to the main route to Wolseley. Now that we have neighbours, we have a common trail we use."

"Neighbours?" Emily asked, surprised.

"Yes, there must be twenty families or so in the area. Some folks from back home have joined us."

"I guess I hadn't noticed." She'd have to take a closer look across the landscape on her return.

Geordie continued his explanation. "It's also a nice flat spot, sheltered from the wind."

"Yes, it is," Emily agreed as they caught sight of the proud stone house surrounded by a nest of chokecherry bushes and green ash to the south, and caragana on the west. Poplar bluffs rimmed the other sides of the yard. The house's grandeur was already evident.

"You sure work fast," she noted, amazed to see how much of the stonework was completed, and that they'd started on the rafters.

Geordie looked at her in surprise. "You haven't been here since last Tuesday."

"Oh, no," she said. "Your time goes by so much faster than mine. It was only yesterday for me. That explains why things have changed so much. Four years have passed for you, but for me, it's only been three months."

Geordie looked at her in astonishment.

"Good thing my time doesn't change too much while I'm here," she added.

"Come on then," Geordie called, striding towards the house. "Time's a-wasting."

They skirted the remaining piles of sand and stones, passing masonry tools, and ducking under scaffolding. Geordie led her up a plank to the main door. She stared in awe at the freshly placed stones of the wall, running her hands over them. Stepping inside, she felt the instant coolness of the somewhat hollow interior.

"The kitchen," she said.

The sunlight streamed through several windows criss-crossing the wood floors in the open expanse. There were no interior walls yet, only the supporting posts and beams.

"Yes," Geordie answered. Then he pointed out where the other rooms would be as they toured the first floor. "The parlour will be over there, and a smaller bed-sitting room next to it."

Emily recognized the space as the current living room and the office.

"And this will be the dining room," Geordie continued.

"Where's the fireplace?" Emily asked, walking over to the spot where it was in the house now.

He looked warily at her, as if wondering how she could know about something they hadn't already done. "We'll build it once we have the roof on."

Emily nodded. Then she noticed the stairs.

"Careful," he cautioned. "The railing isn't on yet."

"No problem," she said, scampering upwards without hesitation. "They don't squeak," she said after a few moments.

Geordie seemed offended. "When the Elliotts build stairs, we build them solid!"

Emily smiled. "They squeak in my time." She pointed out the one that she always avoided when she snuck down them. It was solid now.

Grabbing a hammer and a couple of nails, Geordie pounded them into the tread to make sure it was firmly in place. As they continued up, Emily marvelled at the huge expanse that would be the three bedrooms and the bathroom on the second floor. She named the four rooms as she paced them out.

"Bathroom?" Geordie raised his eyebrows. He listened intently as she explained.

"We'll not being having the likes of that in here." He seemed appalled at the very notion. "We've a sturdy out-building that is more fitting for such coarse things, and the tub in front of the kitchen stove suits us fine. This is a bedroom."

Emily chuckled at his olden-days notions. She let the subject drop, excited now to be near the top. She entered the attic. A large wooden beam stretched above her down the centre ridge. From this spanned a few rafters.

"Don't go too close to the edge," Geordie warned.

Ignoring him, Emily went straight to what would be her bedroom, and leaned out of what would be the dormer. As she did so, she glanced down at a window opening on the floor below her. She was surprised to see the width of the stone wall and that it was actually two walls with gravelly rubble in between. She'd never considered the broadness of it before and how the builders might have achieved the sixty-centimetre width. She'd assumed they'd used big rocks, positioning them to the required thickness by staggering smaller rocks in between them for a close fit and filling the spaces with mortar to achieve a plumb, relatively flat surface on the outside and inside of each wall.

"Aye, lass," Geordie noticed her interest. "The wall has two faces. We wanted a good sturdy one."

The scene that greeted her through the window was similar to the one at home. She could see out across the pasture to the outcropping of rocks, although there were more bushes and bluffs blocking the view.

"This is where I sleep," she said, turning to Geordie.

"In the attic?"

She nodded, striding across the newly constructed floor, the smell of fresh lumber mingled with the dampness of mortar and the soft afternoon breeze. Gazing out the opposite window opening, she noted the new henhouse and the enclosure that held the pigs, hidden by trees. Neither of those buildings existed anymore in the farmyard of her current life.

"Well, that's it, then. You've seen it all," Geordie said at her elbow.

"Thank you for showing it to me."

"You're welcome!" he smiled. "Would you like to help me feed the pigs now, then?"

She wrinkled her nose. "Maybe some other time. I must get back."

"Och, you're missing a real treat," he grinned at her.

As they descended, Emily savoured every moment, trying to imprint what she was seeing in her mind, so she could compare it when she got home. Once outside again, she looked up at the stone house, admiring it.

"I can hardly believe I get to see my grandparents' house being built."

"Tell me how they came to own it," Geordie asked, as they began walking across the yard.

Now was as good a time as any to talk about the family relationship, Emily thought, but how should she approach it? "My grandmother grew up in it," she began. "She was the youngest in her family and the last one at home, so when she married she and her husband, my grandfather, took over the house and looked after her father until he passed away."

Geordie listened with rapt attention. "And how did her father come by it?"

Emily paused for a few moments, trying to decide how to tell him. "Well, this is the tricky part," she said, watching his face. "He built it."

"But he couldn't have, my father did..." Geordie's eyes widened. "Do you mean to tell me...?"

Emily nodded. "Yes, we're related."

A shudder ran through Geordie's body as if someone were walking on his grave. "That can't be possible," he said, stepping away in shock.

"It can be and it is," Emily said, gently.

He seemed oblivious to Sorcha, who had just joined them, looking for attention. Staring at Emily in fear, he shook his head. Abruptly, he walked off. Bewildered, the dog followed him.

"You're trying to put some kind of spell on me," he said over his shoulder. "I don't know for what purpose."

"Wait," Emily called, starting after him.

"Just stay away from me," he ordered, quickening his pace.

"Please, just think about it," she pleaded. "How could I possibly know about the fireplace?" Instantly, she knew that was the wrong thing to say.

She watched him head towards the henhouse with Sorcha racing ahead. How could she convince him she meant him no harm? And how could she prove their relationship?

CHAPTER SEVEN

As Geordie put distance between them, Emily turned away sadly. She didn't have time to try to explain and he didn't seem to be in the mood to listen. She trudged home, her shoulders slumped as she thought about her conversation with Geordie, her parent's divorce, and the whole idea of the auction and the loss of so many things tied to her grandmother's life.

When she reached the big rock, she climbed up top and sat looking over the prairies. A slight breeze whispered past her. The morning sun warmed her back and soothed away her unhappiness. She let the peacefulness surround her until she became calm again.

In the marsh, a furry brown muskrat slid into the water and swam to the other side, then disappeared into a mound of reeds and mud. Ducks skidded to a halt on top of the water, and then paddled about. They always made her laugh when they upended, stretching their heads into the water to reach their food.

Peaceful once more, Emily rose and descended to the ground. Gently she placed the oval stone into the crevice of the rock. A sudden thought went through her mind. What if for some reason she got stuck in the past? Would she able to handle it? She decided that although she loved to visit, she wouldn't want to live the rest of her life in those conditions. She couldn't imagine not having running water or an indoor bathroom, or even a grocery store nearby. The very thought of all the hard work they did made her feel tired. She also felt hungry.

Back home, Emily walked around the huge stone house examining it from all directions. A feeling of admiration welled up in her. She came around to the main door to find Aunt Liz standing on the porch watching her.

"Why the sudden interest in the house?" she asked.

Emily joined her aunt on the step. "I guess because we won't be coming back again for a long time."

Aunt Liz seemed to understand how she felt. "So everything is taking on more meaning for you."

"This house is so much part of our heritage," Emily said proudly.

"Yes, it is." Aunt Liz seemed sad.

"Couldn't we keep it somehow?" Emily suddenly realized how important this was to her.

"I'm afraid not, sweetie." Aunt Liz gave her a hug. "You know, we've already made arrangements for Gerald to buy the place."

Suddenly, her mom called from the doorway, "Breakfast is ready."

"Did Mom make it?" Emily asked.

Aunt Liz nodded. Emily groaned. Her mom wasn't the greatest cook in the world.

"It won't be so bad," said Aunt Liz. "It's only cold cereal and toasted bagels."

"Good thing!" Emily went into the kitchen with a grin on her face. She polished off a bowl of Cheerios and a cinnamon raisin bagel with choke-cherry jam.

"You have quite the appetite this morning," her mom commented, passing her the milk.

"A little walk in the morning helps," she admitted.

"Great, then you'll be energized to help carry the boxes out of the veranda and set them on the tables for tomorrow."

Emily's first instinct was to complain, but then she thought of all the work the Elliotts did. Shuffling a few boxes around didn't seem like such hard work compared to hauling stones to build a house. As her mom and aunt set up tables, Emily loaded herself up.

"I think we should set the tables in shorter rows, vertically," Kate suggested. She stood with her hands on her hips and surveyed the tables they'd set up so far.

"That will make it too confusing," Aunt Liz said. "We want people to be able to get around them easily and not have any traffic jams."

"Well, leaving them in one long row makes people have to walk the whole length."

"And what's the problem with that?" Aunt Liz sounded exasperated.

"Well, maybe they don't want to see everything. I think it would be better if we did it in sections."

Emily set her load of boxes on the nearest table and watched her mom and aunt.

"How about a compromise?" Emily suggested. She didn't want to waste any more time.

Aunt Liz looked at Emily in surprise. "Okay, we'll leave them in one row, but leave gaps every few tables so people can get through. Will that satisfy you, Miss Bossy Boots?"

"Fine," Kate answered sourly, snapping the legs up on another folding table. "Just quit calling me that!"

Emily laughed at her mom's childhood nickname.

As she carried more boxes out, Emily wondered what to do about Geordie. She wanted to be his friend, and she'd just have to go back and convince him of that. It didn't matter if he believed they were related or not. When she finished helping with the boxes, she'd go back and try to talk to him.

Gerald and Donald Ferguson arrived about an hour later, along with a couple of other men and one of the auctioneers. Together, they hauled the rest of the smaller equipment, tools, and assorted farm gear out of the Quonset and bins. The auctioneer made suggestions on where to place everything. A cheery atmosphere prevailed, with everyone chatting and calling out instructions. Emily was happy to be part of the group working together, but she felt sad to see all her grandparents' belongings strewn about the yard for all to inspect. She'd give anything to be able to go back to when her grandmother was alive.

By the time Emily finished helping clear out the veranda, it was noon. All the boxes were laid out, but unpacked. They'd do that early the next morning, just before the auctioneers arrived. Overnight, they'd keep them safe from the weather under plastic tarps.

As she worked, Emily had kept alert for anything resembling a small box that would take her small key, but nothing came close. She ambled over to the other side of the yard and inspected everything there, half-heartedly poking into boxes, bins, and buckets of bolts.

"Needing something special?" Donald asked, carrying a paint sprayer from the tool shed.

"No, just taking a last look," she said, not willing to tell him the real reason. "Making sure something isn't getting sold that I might want," she added with a grin.

"Don't let your mom hear you say that!" he laughed, setting the paint sprayer in place on the ground.

"Has she been talking to you about me?" asked Emily annoyed.

"No, ma'am," he grinned. "I just know what she's like."

"You seem to know her pretty well," Emily fished for more information.

"Somewhat. We dated in high school," said Donald, heading back into the shed. He emerged with a box of nozzles, hoses, and other gadgets.

High school sweethearts. Emily wrinkled up her nose at the thought. Somehow, she couldn't picture her mom as a carefree teenager with a boyfriend like Donald. She seemed too serious for that.

"How long did you go out?" asked Emily.

"Three or four years. Right up until we both left for university." He wound the cord back around the paint sprayer.

Emily sat on the edge of a stack of boards. "Couldn't you continue to see each other?" she asked, not bothering to hide her curiosity.

"We moved to different cities at opposite ends of the country," he answered.

"You still could have written and seen each other on holidays. What happened?"

"Your dad happened," Donald shrugged his shoulders.

"Oh." Emily didn't know what else to say.

"Life's like that sometimes," he said, straightening up.

Suddenly, Emily heard her name called.

"Don't talk Donald's ear off, Emily," her mom called across the yard. "We could use your help with lunch."

"Coming," Emily replied, relieved at escaping from an uncomfortable situation. She turned to Donald, "See you later."

He nodded and headed back into the shed.

With the five men joining them in the kitchen for lunch, Emily could easily observe Donald and her mom without being noticed. They seemed to be doing their best to avoid each other, although she did catch them eyeing one another across the table. Once Donald caught Kate looking at him and she glanced away, her face flushing. For two people who hadn't seen each other in a long time, they sure were keeping track of one another. Emily decided she'd ask Aunt Liz more about their early romance. Her mom probably wouldn't tell her.

As they cleaned up the kitchen, Emily had other thoughts on her mind. She waited until they were alone, then she approached her mom, "Mom, is there any way we could keep this house?"

Astonished, Kate stared at her. "Of course not! Whatever would you want to do that for?"

"It's special. Your grandfather built it. You grew up here. We should keep it in the family." Emily felt the pride growing inside her again.

Kate groaned. "Emily we've been through all this before. We have to let this place go!"

"I know we can't keep up with the farm, and Gerald's letting us use the house for a while. But why couldn't we buy it back from him? You know, just keep the house and the yard."

"We can't afford the upkeep. And you know none of us has the time to worry about the place." Kate seemed exasperated. "Subject closed!"

Deflated, Emily dried the dishes without another word. Aunt Liz, who had just entered the room, avoided looking at either of them.

Finally, Kate broke the silence. "How are you doing with finding the box that fits the key?"

"Not so good," Emily admitted. "I don't know where to look. Do you have any ideas?"

"None so far," said her mom, wiping off the counters.

"He probably hid it somewhere and forgot where," Aunt Liz teased.

"You know, that's a possibility," said Kate.

"You're a genius," Emily added.

"Not quite," Aunt Liz said. "Just because he built secret compartments in desks, doesn't mean he hid the box."

"But it makes sense, doesn't it?" asked Emily. "We already know it can't be anywhere out in the open. We've sorted, cleaned, packed, moved, and otherwise gone over this entire house centimetre by centimetre."

"True!" Aunt Liz agreed.

Suddenly Emily thought about the outbuildings. "Would he have hidden it outside somewhere?"

"I doubt it," said her mom.

"He would have been more careful than that," Aunt Liz agreed.

"Well, do you have ideas where it might be, then?"

Jokingly, her mom said, "Let's just hope he didn't hide it behind a stone like in one of those old English mysteries!"

Aunt Liz groaned. "Could you imagine trying to find a loose stone in this big house?"

The two of them started to laugh, but Emily interrupted them.

"That's not such a far-fetched idea," Emily said seriously. "It would make sense wouldn't it?"

Thoughtfully, they considered the options.

"Well, it wouldn't be just any old stone," Aunt Liz said. "It would have to be in a special, well-thought-out place. That's the kind of man he was."

"I didn't know him," said Kate.

"Really?" Emily looked at her mother, hoping she'd continue.

"No, he died just after I was born."

"Yes, I was quite young when he died, and I'm ten years older than your mom," Aunt Liz confirmed.

"Do you have any of these dates written down anywhere?" asked Emily.

Her mom shook her head, looking over at Aunt Liz.

"Not that I know of," Aunt Liz said, thinking hard. "But you know, if anyone knew if there was any hidden place, it would be your Aunt Maggie."

"Let's call her," Emily said.

Aunt Liz smiled. "No can do. She's in New Zealand for another two weeks."

"Darn," said Emily. "Isn't there anyone else?"

"No," said her mom. "No one else took any interest in the family history."

"Maybe Uncle Ian would know about a hiding place?"

"We can ask him," her mom agreed. "But we'll have to do it later. We have to slip into town now and pick up those supplies for serving coffee at the auction tomorrow."

"Agreed," said Aunt Liz. "So much for an early morning start. If we don't get a move on right now, the stores will be closing for the night."

"Do you have the list?" asked Kate, searching for her car keys.

Aunt Liz nodded, grabbing it off the kitchen counter.

Before Emily had a chance to ask if she could give Uncle Ian a call, they were already out the door.

"Make sure you stay put, Emily," her mom called as she got into the car.

Emily didn't respond. She watched them drive out of the yard, followed shortly afterwards by the Fergusons and the other men. Now was her chance to make a quick trip back to the past and deal with Geordie. She had to make him understand their connection. Even if he wouldn't believe it, he had to realize that she was his friend.

At the outcropping of rocks, Emily braced herself for her talk with Geordie. She thought about showing him their family photograph, but he'd just say she'd found it in the house somewhere. All she could do was try to explain the situation to him. If he didn't believe her, there was nothing else she could do.

She used the stone and the sentinel rock to transport herself back to the past, then slid the stone into her pocket. Stumbling over the uneven ground, she headed to the sod homestead site first. Even before she arrived, she knew the family wasn't there. Quickly, she followed the path behind the barn and aimed for the stone house, wondering what she might say to Geordie. Would he even acknowledge her?

When she reached the crest of the hill, she was astonished to see the exterior walls and roof of the house finished. Although there was no glass in the windows, the shutters were attached. Forms made of rough planks for building the stone steps were in place. She couldn't make out who they were, but two of the men worked on levelling them. She could hear hammering inside.

She slid behind a stand of trees situated halfway to the house and peered about. In the distance, on the south side of the house, she noticed a garden with figures bending over the plants. Just beyond it was a field of corn and a huge potato patch. She moved closer for a better look.

The two youngest girls, Katie and Beth, were picking peas into wooden pails, while Bella and Geordie's mom sat in the shade of a poplar tree and shelled them into a huge tin bowl. Then Emily noticed another little person bobbing through the cornfield, and she knew it was Molly. Emily drew back behind the corner of the house, so Molly wouldn't see her and cause a fuss while the others were around. Obviously there was no way she was going to see her alone this time. Ducking around to the other side of the house, she watched Geordie's dad and oldest brother Sandy working on the steps for a while.

Then she skulked around to the back door, carefully climbing up an inclined plank to peer inside. Jack and Duncan had two kitchen walls completely framed. She watched as they worked on the dining room.

A few minutes later, she realized they were constructing the framework for the fireplace. Fascinated, she observed them as they worked, running floor joists close together under the base to support the weight of the stones that would later be added. At one point, they cut one of the joists shorter, so that it didn't come out all the way, which left a wider opening at the front, almost as if they were leaving a gap on purpose. They seemed to be assembling some kind of enclosure inside it. Perhaps it was for an air vent of some kind. She leaned in for a better view.

All at once, she felt the plank sway beneath her. Her breath caught in her throat as she looked around and saw Geordie lifting the other end. He gave the board a little wiggle, then set it down again. Emily felt all her muscles tighten. But when he looked up at her, he smiled. She relaxed.

"Trying to make me walk the gangplank?" she asked playfully.

"Who's there?" Duncan asked from inside.

Geordie and Emily froze.

"I am," Geordie answered.

"Well, quit fooling around and do some work," Jack called to him.

Geordie motioned for Emily to follow him. They dashed around the corner of the house and he led her behind the caragana bushes where they wouldn't be overheard. They didn't say a word until they were out of sight.

"I'm glad you came back," he said.

"I couldn't stay away," she said, happy that he was speaking to her again. "I didn't mean to upset you."

"I do apologize for the way I treated you a few days ago," Geordie said, "so let's not talk about it again."

"Apology accepted. But you said a few days ago? It was just this morning in my time." This worried her. "There don't seem to be any rules about the way time changes here compared to my life," she complained.

"I'm happy to see you whenever you come," said Geordie.

Emily shook her head, "But I can never plan anything."

"We don't usually do anything special," he said. "Although, my brother Sandy is getting married at the end of the week. You might find that a wee bit of fun."

"Oh, yes, I'd love to be here," said Emily. "But we'd have to figure out when I needed to come."

"The wedding takes place mid-afternoon, and we have to travel to the bride's home, so you'd need to be here no later than noon four days from now."

They compared the various times she'd shown up in Geordie's world to when she'd left hers. Time in Geordie's life seemed to have slowed down since she'd begun interacting with him. The three-months-to-four-year ratio wasn't the same anymore. The closest they could figure out was that half a day in Emily's life was about four days in Geordie's.

"I'd have to come back tomorrow morning," she gasped. "But I can't. The farm auction is tomorrow. I have to help and I want to be there. This is terrible. I really want to be here, too."

Geordie looked disappointed. "It would be fun to have you here, lass, but if it's not meant to be, there is nothing we can do about it."

"I'll figure out how to get here somehow," Emily

declared. "If only I had some way of getting right to this spot." She turned away. "I must go now."

"Wait," Geordie said. "I've been thinking about what you said about us being related and all. I don't know if it's right or not, or how that could be possible, but I know Emma trusted you."

Emily turned back to him. "I'm so glad to hear you say that!"

Geordie continued, "I was also thinking about the way you come and go, and, well, if a stone Emma gave you worked, maybe if I gave you something, you could come back easily right here to this house."

"What did you have in mind?" she asked, excitement dancing in her eyes.

"I made you this," Geordie pulled a whittled piece of wood from his pocket.

"It's beautiful," Emily took the tiny bird-shaped carving from him. "But how will it work?"

"It's only a thought, mind, but seeing as how we are both connected to the stone house, I wondered if we hid it somewhere at the house it might work?"

"What a great idea! But where?" Emily turned to look at the house.

"I know the perfect place. Follow me," said Geordie, adding, "But don't say a word until we get there."

Emily nodded okay.

CHAPTER EIGHT

Emily followed Geordie as they made their way back towards the house. They stayed out of his family's view as much as possible.

"They'll give me more little tasks to do, if they catch sight of me," he whispered as they made their way around the bushes. "They're always giving me the simple ones that even the girls could manage," he added with some annoyance.

As they trekked across the yard, Emily watched the two men working on the front stone step. As she came closer, she saw that George Sr. was one of the workers, but she didn't recognize the other man. Was this William Gibson, the stonemason she'd heard about? She watched as they chose stones and cleaned them off, carefully examining them first before setting them into place.

"What are they doing?" Emily whispered as she caught up to Geordie at the corner of the house.

"Looking for the ones with the smoothest tops and those without any hairline cracks," Geordie answered softly.

Emily stood transfixed at the sight. The men used a series of chisels and hammers to cut the stones so they were the right shape to fit into the plank form. They worked on their knees, chiselling the stones on the soft ground, making one side of each flat for the top of the step.

"How can they cut right through rock?"

"If they take their time chiselling along a line, the stone will crack where they want it to, and they can also cut along the grain of the stone," Geordie explained. "I'd give anything to be helping them do that," he added, before he disappeared around the side of the house.

Emily stayed where she was to watch. As the men positioned the stones in the mortar, they checked to make sure they were level, using a taut rope strung out along the length of each step as a guide. They used smaller pieces of rock to shim the stones into place.

Pulling herself away from the stonemasonry, Emily scurried after Geordie. When she reached him, she found him kneeling beside the foundation near the back doorway. He was yanking at a length of a small tree limb stuck into the dried mortar of the wall. Puzzled, Emily waited until Geordie managed to dislodge the piece of wood, leaving a two-and-a-half-centimetre-round hole in the wall, just about the size of a broom handle.

"There," Geordie said, standing up and pointing. "How's that for a good place to hide the carving?"

Emily nodded and placed the wooden bird inside. It nestled perfectly, hidden from view. Looking up at Geordie, she asked, "What is this hole for?"

"It's an air vent," he explained. "We have them every few feet."

That's when Emily noticed small limbs protruding all along the foundation. She'd never noticed any of these holes in her grandmother's house.

"Won't someone notice this one's open?" Emily asked.

"Not if I clean the rest of them out," he said confidently. "It has to be done anyway."

Suddenly, they heard voices from around the corner of the house. Emily and Geordie squeezed tight against the wall.

"I won't do it," Beth's voice came to them.

"Come on," whined Kate. "Mum says you must."

"Well, I think it's a waste!" Beth said.

"Girls, stop being contrary and get on with it!" Geordie's mom quelled the argument.

"It's Beth, Mum," Kate replied. "She doesn't want to sort the carrots."

"Beth, do you always have to be so disagreeable?" her mom asked.

"But she wants us to line them all up by their size," Beth protested.

"Kate," their mother chuckled, "there is no need to be so particular!"

"Oh, all right," Kate said, "but then they won't be sorted proper."

"I'll sort them," Beth said sullenly. "But I'm not lining them up. They're going in piles." Their voices came from farther away.

"Bring the buckets over here, then," Kate said.

"No, you do it yourself," Beth said.

Kate scolded, "Why can't you just do things the way I tell you to?"

"Kate," their mom called out, "try not to be so bossy!"

There were a few moments of silence, and then they could hear Kate hissing at Beth. "You're always getting me into trouble with Mum."

Emily raised her eyes at Geordie in a silent question when they'd gone.

Geordie shrugged his shoulders. "Kate always wants to do things her way. We call her Miss Bossy Boots."

Emily smiled, thinking about how Aunt Liz had called her mom that very same thing. No wonder her mom was named after her. The two Kates even argued the same way!

"Do you really think this will work?" she asked, giving her attention back to Geordie.

"All we can do is try," he answered, plucking the little carving out of its hiding place and holding it gently in his hands.

"It's not going to work if I'm still holding the stone," Emily guessed.

"Do you need to leave it at the rock?" Geordie wondered.

"I'm not sure," Emily admitted with some alarm. "I've never left it anywhere else before. And if I do now, I don't know if I'll be able to find it again and get back here."

Geordie considered the options and then with a slight flush said, "I could repeat what I did before."

Dawning realization crossed Emily's face. "Of course! When you took it from the rock, I couldn't get back, but then it showed up under the windowsill in the bag of stones, where I found it again."

Geordie shook his head. "I didn't put the stone there, but I could this time."

A stab of fear ran through Emily. "How did they get there?"

"I don't know. Molly's to have Emma's pouch of stones when she's older. Mum said so."

Suddenly, Molly appeared suddenly beside them. "What am I to have?"

Her face was all rosy, as if she'd been running, and one side of her dark, plaited hair was coming undone. Neither Geordie nor Emily said anything for several moments. This was the first time Emily had seen her so closely. She was tanned from being outdoors, and she had a very strong lilt to her voice.

"What are you two talking about?" she asked, looking straight at Emily with curiosity. "And who are you?"

Emily laughed, and knelt down to have a better look at the impish four-year-old with the twinkling, bright blue eyes and the freckled face. Emily remembered that when she was little, she'd had freckles too. Her gran had called them "sun-kisses."

"Hello, Molly." She took her hand and gave it a gentle shake. "My name is Emily."

Molly gave her a wide grin. "How do you do?" she asked politely, not one bit shy. "Would you like to come and see my dwelling in the trees?" Her voice sparkled with enthusiasm and wonder.

Emily looked up at Geordie for a brief moment. Geordie shrugged his shoulders.

"I would love to see it," Emily said, taking her by the hand, not wanting to pass this opportunity to spend some time with her grandmother as a child.

"I'll just stay here and clean out these vents," suggested Geordie, obviously not interested in any make-believe place.

Molly led her to the other side of the caragana bushes and a little ways over the meadow towards a stand of poplar. Emily kept careful watch to make sure they weren't observed, but everyone seemed intent on their tasks. As they traipsed over the pasture, Molly picked buffalo beans, bluebells, paintbrush, and some little white blossoms, handing them to Emily until she held a bright bouquet of wildflowers. Emily's chest became tight with longing and sadness as Molly chatted and pointed out the birds and the gophers diving for cover. She thought again of the last times she'd spent with her aging grandmother, walking this very same land.

After some time, they reached the bluff. Before entering the trees, Molly slipped her hand into Emily's, and they stood silently looking over the landscape. Emily was barely able to breathe, feeling the fragility of the moment of connection to her grandmother, wishing it would never end.

A moment later, Molly looked up at her and smiled, then tugged her towards the trees.

"Isn't this too far away from the house?" asked Emily with sudden realization, and alarmed by the distance they had come. "Maybe you should stay closer to your family where they can see you and take care of you."

"I'm not in danger here," Molly said, looking out over the grassy meadow filled with autumn flowers and purple vetch. "The meadow fairies will take care of me."

Emily felt a shiver of knowing go up her back, and a peacefulness came over her as the two of them connected with the prairie, the wind, the sky, and all that was around them. A bubbling *bob-o-link* song repeated several times in the sky over the meadow. And, although she wasn't sure, Emily thought an eagle soared way overhead.

"This is where Jane sleeps," Molly parted some low bushes and put her finger to her lips. "Sshhh."

She showed Emily a soft bed of leafy branches suspended thirty centimetres above the underbrush, with a piece of a burlap sack for a mattress and an old cloth for a blanket, wrapped around a small porcelain-faced doll.

"You have a lovely baby," Emily whispered.

Molly nodded and motioned her back to another section of the trees, guiding her around the imaginary rooms of the house. Bunches of brilliantly coloured flowers decorated some of the lower boughs, indicating the passageways. She showed Emily the windows she'd fashioned through the branches. Emily followed, thrilled to be with her and to be seeing how her grandmother had been as a little girl, playing in her fantasy world. Molly at last pointed out the kitchen with its low tree stumps for chairs and invited her for tea.

"Thank you," Emily said to Molly politely, "but I must decline, as I need to get home now."

Molly cocked her head to one side as if listening to someone speak. "Yes, your mother is looking for you," she said. "She says you are very late."

Emily nodded her head. "It's probably time you were back, too," she said.

"Let's run then," said Molly, taking Emily's hand and dragging her out of the trees.

Molly laughed and chattered along the way. As they neared the house, Geordie joined them.

"Come here, half-pint." Geordie swung her up on his shoulders and they jogged to the rear of the stone house. Moments later, she slid to the ground by the back door.

"Bye, Emily," she said, stepping over to give Emily a hug.

Emily felt an overwhelming sense of tenderness that threatened to dissolve into tears.

"Don't be sad," Molly said. "I'll see you again." Then she skipped off and disappeared around the corner of the house.

"Molly, where have you been?" they heard her sister Kate asking. "You must stop your gallivanting all over. And look at you. Your hair is all undone. Come. Let me tidy your braids."

Emily and Geordie chuckled quietly to themselves. Then they turned to Emily's problem of whether to go home by Geordie's proposed new way. He held out the carved bird.

Shaking off her sense of contentment, Emily wondered if taking the bird would work to get her back and forth in time, as the stones did. Or did the stones only work because Molly had grown up with them? What a dilemma! She didn't know what to do.

"We must think this through carefully. I want to be able to come back to visit you for sure."

She had so many things she wanted to accomplish when she came again to pioneer time. Besides seeing the stone house finished, and wanting to know more about their lives, she needed to come back to see if she could figure out where her great-grandfather might have concealed the special box. Most of all, she wanted to spend more time with Molly.

"I can't stay any longer right now, so I'll go my usual way," she said, realizing that she needed to get back home immediately. "But I'll come again as soon as I can."

"Here, at least take the carving with you," Geordie thrust it into her hand.

"No, I mustn't," she said, giving it back. Her mind seemed to suddenly clear. "Put it into the hiding place," she said firmly. "I'll see if I can find it when I'm home. If it doesn't work, we'll have to figure out something the next time I come back."

Reluctantly, Geordie returned the carved bird into the hiding place. "You will come back for Sandy's wedding?" Geordie asked earnestly.

Emily nodded. "I'll try," she said, before hurrying across the prairie.

As she ran for home, she thought again of the wedding. It would be so much fun to see an old-fashioned one. But she also wanted to attend the farm auction. It would be a farewell to her grandmother's home the way she'd known it. How was she going to manage both? If only she could use Geordie's carving to travel directly to the stone house.

When she returned to the farmyard, she glanced quickly about to see if anyone was around. Then she strode to the house, peering at the foundation. There they were – small round holes several centimetres apart that she'd never noticed before. These had fine screen across them, probably to keep out rodents and bugs.

Reaching the back of the house, she worked out where the hole with the carving should be, near the back door, and found it covered with plants. Kneeling in the flower bed, she pushed aside the geraniums and hollyhocks to reach the foundation wall. The hole was there.

"What are you doing, Emily?" Her mom startled her, coming around the corner.

Emily let the flowers go and jumped to her feet.

"You've either taken a very sudden interest in gardening, or you have a weird fascination for stone walls," her mom continued.

"Uh, I was just looking at the construction," Emily said quickly, brushing the dirt off her knees.

"And you're in the flower bed because?" Kate asked, perplexed.

Emily ignored the direct question. "Did you know this house has rough-faced walls? They weren't all built the same."

"I never thought about it," Kate said matter-of-factly.

"Some of them were built with smoother surfaces," Emily edged her way past her mother, hoping to lead her away from the special hole in the foundation.

"I suppose Donald's been filling your head full of stone building facts!"

"I'm just interested, is all," Emily said, hoping to avoid any further discussion.

"Well, I guess it can't hurt," said her mom.

Emily tried to change the subject. "Can we call Uncle Ian now?"

"We already did," said her mom. "We couldn't find you when we came back. I thought I told you to stay put!"

"I was here all the time," Emily said, crossing her fingers behind her back as she told her not-quite lie. She really had been here at the house, so that part was at least true.

"Well, we couldn't find you!"

"I was probably just poking around somewhere," Emily suggested.

Kate shook her head. "You must stop gallivanting all over!"

Emily walked ahead with a hint of smile on her face as she recalled Kate in the past saying the very same thing to Molly. "So what did Uncle Ian say?"

"He wasn't there. I left a message," said her mom.

"Then, can I call Dad now?"

"Give it another hour – until after six – so it's cheaper," her mom called out to her retreating back. "You can help get supper on!"

Emily let the screen door slam as she entered the veranda. Do this, do that; her mom was always so bossy!

Her scowl disappeared when she remembered the exchange between Kate and Beth in the past. Things didn't seem to have changed much from one life to another.

When she at last telephoned her dad, Emily found him in a good mood.

"We just heard that we've secured some substantial grants for our new research project," she heard him say.

"Wonderful, Dad," Emily responded. "Does that mean you'll be home more, so I can visit?"

"Well, sorry pumpkin, but I'll actually have to travel more often for a while, gathering all the samples and materials,"

"When will I see you, then?" she asked, feeling a lump growing in her throat.

Hesitantly, he answered, "I'm not sure, Em, but as soon as I'm done the bulk of the exploration, I could take some time off. We could take a little holiday together, say in a couple of months. How would that be?"

A huge disappointed sigh escaped from Emily before she could stop it. She felt her eyes watering, and she clutched the phone.

"Okay, Dad," she said, trying not to let her voice crack.

"Great!" Apparently he hadn't noticed the sigh.

"I have to go now, Dad," she said quickly. "Aunt Liz needs to use the phone." She gave him the first excuse that came to her mind.

"Well, all right, then," he sounded surprised. "I'll talk to you again soon, okay, Emily?"

"Okay," she said quietly.

"I love you, pumpkin," her dad ended on an upbeat note, although she thought she detected a little sadness too.

"Love you too, Dad," Emily said, her voice breaking. She hung up the phone and went upstairs, before anyone could see her.

She only made it to the second floor before the ache in her throat gave way. Going into the bathroom, she closed the door and burst into tears. She wasn't important in her dad's life. She wouldn't see much of him from now on, she just knew it. Why did her parents have to divorce? Her whole life was wretched.

"Emily?" her mother's voice came from the other side of the door. "Are you all right?"

Hurriedly, she mopped at her eyes with a towel.

"I'm okay," Emily's voice came out muffled.

"Are you sure?" her mom asked quietly. "Can I come in?"

"I'll be out in a minute."

"Let me see you," persisted her mother.

"Just give me a couple of minutes," Emily turned on the tap and splashed her face with water. "I'll be right down."

"Okay, then."

She heard her mom going downstairs.

When she stepped into the kitchen, her mom and aunt looked at her with concern. Emily grabbed a tea towel and began drying forks and knives. She fumbled them into the utensil drawer, unable to see clearly. She kept her head down as she worked, letting her hair fall into her face.

"What did your dad say?" her mom asked from across the kitchen, obviously trying to decide whether to come to her or not.

"He's too busy to see me." She took a deep breath. "He's going on a research trip for two months."

As Emily brushed past her mom, she struggled to keep her emotions in check. Her mom reached out and put her arm around her shoulders, holding her close. Emily tried to think of other things, looking out the window at the sun lowering on the horizon, looking at the clock ticking, anything to keep from breaking down again.

Emily felt her mom's chin resting on the top of her head, as she whispered, "I'm sorry, Em."

"I'm okay, Mom," she said, breaking away and returning to dry the glasses sitting on the drainboard.

As Aunt Liz washed the plates in the sink next to her, Emily felt her nose begin to run. She swiped at it with her hand, struggling to keep her mind occupied. All of a sudden, tears blinded her and she couldn't see the plates she was reaching for.

"Aw, sweetie," Aunt Liz grabbed the tea towel and quickly wiped the suds off her hands, then gathered Emily into her arms. She hugged her tightly.

Emily blubbered into her aunt's shoulder, as her mom snatched up several Kleenexes and pressed them into her hands. She dabbed at Emily's eyes, and brushed her hair soothingly out of her face.

"Come sit down," Kate tugged her gently towards the table, and hastily drew a chair out for her.

Emily let her mom and aunt coddle her. Her mom pulled out another chair and sat close to her, while Aunt Liz brought her a glass of water.

"Just because he's got work to do, doesn't mean he doesn't care," Kate said softly.

"I know," Emily nodded her head and blew her nose. "I just wanted to see him."

Kate gave her some fresh tissues. "I know, Em, but you can phone him lots."

"Okay," Emily said, knowing it wasn't the same thing, but that it was the best that could be done.

Feeling more subdued, she wiped her eyes, gave her nose another blow and took a long sip of water. Then she smiled at her mom and aunt. "I'll be fine."

She stood up.

"That's my girl!" her mom patted her on the shoulders.

Aunt Liz handed the tea towel back to her with a grin.

"Sympathy doesn't get me out of the dishes, huh?"

"Nice try," said her aunt, laughing.

Although Emily still felt a deep sadness, she also felt comforted by the closeness of the three of them as they worked in the kitchen together.

"Guess we'll have to be up by dawn to make sure everything is ready for the auction tomorrow," her mom broke the silence.

"Not a problem," said Emily, glad to be thinking of something else.

"Could you be the gofer between us all tomorrow?" Aunt Liz asked kindly.

"Uh, I guess so," Emily said, half-heartedly. How would she ever escape to the past if they kept her constantly busy? She wanted to go to Sandy's wedding. "What would I have to do?"

"Just make sure the women serving the lunch don't need anything, maybe run messages back and forth between the auctioneers and us," said Aunt Liz.

"Just as long as I get to see everything going on," Emily added, realizing that she didn't want to miss anything, anywhere. How was she going to be in two places at once?

The ringing of the telephone cut into their conversation.

"Ian, how nice to hear your voice," Aunt Liz said.

Hanging up the tea towel, Emily listened while her aunt explained to Uncle Ian about the key and the missing box. He was several years older than Aunt Liz and Aunt Maggie.

"You remember? Wonderful!" Aunt Liz listened some more.

Emily felt her pulse quicken. Her mom moved in closer, trying to eavesdrop.

"I had no idea!" Aunt Liz talked for a few more moments, and then handed the phone to Kate.

"There's a loose stone in the fireplace in the living room," Aunt Liz whispered.

Excitement bubbled inside Emily as she danced towards the hallway. Kate quickly ended the conversation, eyeing Emily and Aunt Liz as they headed to the living room.

"Wait up, you two!" Kate caught up to them just as they reached the fireplace.

"He said it's..." Aunt Liz stopped abruptly as Emily dropped to her knees.

She'd suddenly remembered the extra space Jack and Duncan had left in the base of the fireplace as they were building it. She knew exactly which spot it should be in. Would the hidden box be there?

CHAPTER NINE

"Emily, how could you know where to look?" Aunt Liz asked her sharply, dropping to the floor beside her.

"Just a good guess," Emily said as she pushed on one of the stones.

"You are one strange kid," Aunt Liz squeezed in beside her.

Her mom knelt on the other side, looking at a fine crack in the mortar around one of the stones. "It has to be right here, about where Emily is."

"It probably hasn't been moved for years. I don't recall Mom or Dad ever showing us this or opening it," said Aunt Liz.

They struggled to move the stone, but nothing worked.

"Maybe we need a crowbar?" suggested Kate.

"No," Emily exclaimed. "That would wreck it!"

"I think she's right," Aunt Liz said. "There don't seem to be any pry marks on the surface."

"It's another one of those mystery latches, I suppose," Kate said in exasperation.

Emily moved along the base of the fireplace, pushing and prodding all the stones, but nothing budged the one she knew covered the secret opening.

"Maybe Ian was wrong!" Kate said, sitting back on her heels.

"He seemed pretty certain," said Aunt Liz, tapping at the stones.

"This has to be it!" Emily declared.

"How could you know that?" Kate demanded.

"I just do!" Emily wasn't about to explain.

They searched every inch of the fireplace, on the surface, on the mantel, and inside the firebox, looking for some kind of latch or trigger, but after another half-hour passed, they gave up.

"Maybe we should call Ian again," Kate suggested.

"He told us all he knew," said Aunt Liz. "He had no idea how it worked, just where it was supposed to be. He doesn't even know if there's anything inside it."

Emily groaned. Wasn't anyone in her family curious? How could they not know some of these things? She stared again at the fireplace. Everything was solid and immovable. How had her great-grandfather designed the hidden space? All at once, Emily's face brightened. She could go back in time and find out.

"Maybe it's written down somewhere," proposed Aunt Liz.

"We went through all the papers quite thoroughly," Kate answered. "I don't see how we'd have missed something like that."

"Maybe because we weren't looking for it," Aunt Liz chided. "I know exactly where the papers are. I'll get them."

Kate followed Aunt Liz out of the room to a second-floor bedroom. Emily had other plans.

"I'm going out for a walk before bed," she called up to them, determined to find out how to open the hidden compartment. She just hoped the new plan would work to get her there faster.

"Don't be gone long!" her mother yelled back.

I don't plan on it, Emily thought to herself as she whisked out the door and headed for the special hole in the foundation. She didn't waste any time, grubbing through the flower bed getting to the wall in search of Geordie's carved bird.

She peered into the dark hole and at first saw nothing. Picking up a small stick from the ground, she prodded gently inside. If the bird was there, she didn't want to come into direct contact with it. She wanted to be prepared in case she went shooting back into the past. At last, she felt the stick nudge something. She wiggled it towards her, holding her breath in anticipation, as the object neared the edge. She gasped in surprise.

Yes, it was the carved bird, but it was dull-looking, greyed and weathered – not at all like the fresh carving she had seen earlier. Of course, it had been there for nearly a century, so she shouldn't be surprised.

She focused on her immediate task. Rubbing her hands on her jeans, she licked her lips and steadied herself, touching the house for support. Then she reached out and grasped the small carving. At the same time, she lost her footing and fell backwards. She landed on her butt and let out a little screech. She was looking at the same stone wall of the house, but she was in the past, sitting in the rubble and dirt surrounding the construction site, in the twilight.

Quickly, she got to her feet and looked about. She shook the debris off and crept around to the front of the house, looking for signs of human life. As she rounded the last corner, she heard a low whistle, almost like a birdcall. Peering through the dusk, she made out the dim figure of Geordie at the pigpen, waving to her.

As she walked across the yard, she admired the workmanship of the willow branches tightly woven into a fence that held the pigs in their pen. How simple, she thought, realizing they didn't have access to any kind of wire fencing. She laughed quietly over the grunting of the pigs as they rooted at their feed in the trough, reaching Geordie moments later.

"Your plan worked!" she said.

"I'm so glad, lass! And so is Sorcha."

The dog had appeared from the shadows, licking Emily's hands and looking as if she'd welcome a run across the prairie.

"You're a good dog," Emily said, stroking her head. "I wonder how you got your name."

"Sorcha means 'radiant,'" Geordie said. "She's got that little bit of gold in her coat – like a streak of sun."

"That's a wonderful name," Emily said.

"And your first word of Gaelic," Geordie said. "But you're too early for the wedding. It's not for two more days."

"I know," she said breathlessly. "I came to ask you a question."

"Ask me, then." He grinned at her, perching on the step that led into the pig shelter. "As you can see, I'm doing my favourite work."

Emily grinned at him. "You'll be doing harder work soon enough, I'd guess, with Sandy getting married," she said.

"Aye, you may be right." Geordie tapped the space on the step beside him. "But I have two more older brothers, and they are almost finished the house, so I don't suppose they'll give me anything important to do."

Emily sat beside him, absently patting the dog. "I need to know about the secret hiding place in the fire-place," she said. "How does it work?"

Geordie laughed. "How do you know about it? We haven't even finished it yet."

"But you will, and you must know how it's going to work!" Emily insisted.

"Not really, lass," he said. "My dad is a secretive person; he's still working out the details and not likely to tell me."

"Could we take a look? Maybe we could figure it out."

Geordie shrugged his shoulders. "I suppose, but I don't think there is much to see." They walked towards the house.

"Where is the rest of the family? Inside?"

"No, they've gone home for supper, except for..."

Emily shrieked as Kate came around the corner. She had almost walked into her. Sorcha barked and circled Kate. Thank goodness they hadn't collided. Emily didn't know what would have happened, and she didn't want to.

"Geordie, are you talking to ghosts now?" Kate asked peering around.

Geordie shook his head and dropped his hand to his side. Emily kept still, not moving a muscle. Sorcha licked her hand. Emily shook her head, but of course it had no effect.

"Well, come on then, I've finished with those blasted chickens."

Emily knew Kate meant she'd been shooing the last of the chickens inside the henhouse, before closing them in for the night.

"I want to check that the house is secure, and then I'll come," he said dismissing his sister.

"Come now," she said, "the house is fine, and don't you know it. Mum will be crosser than a disturbed wood grouse if we're late for supper again."

Geordie looked out of the corner of his eye at Emily. She shrugged her shoulders and mouthed, "Go."

Geordie sighed. "Can't a man do anything without being ordered around?"

"First, you're not a man," Kate chuckled, "and second, what's so important?"

In the dim light, Emily could see Geordie blush. "You're overstepping your bounds, little lass," he said with a touch of annoyance.

"What would you have me do?" She stood with her hands on her hips.

"Be a little more respectful of your elders," he suggested.

"Ha! You're not much older than me! Besides, what difference does it make how I behave?"

"You'll mind one day," he said. "What man wants a sharp-tongued lass for a wife?"

"Bosh," Kate flung her head back. "As if I'm worried about that. Besides, what lass wants a man who pays her no mind?" she parried. "Whether I tell you straight out or I'm all fancy about it, it comes down to the same thing. We have to get home. I don't see anything that needs to be done that can't wait until tomorrow."

Geordie gave in. "Fine, Miss Bossy Boots. I'll agree with you for the moment – there's nothing that can't wait for a little while longer," he answered. "Whatever needs to be done, I'll do tomorrow, and that's a promise," he added, pointedly looking at Emily.

Emily nodded, understanding that his last words were for her.

Geordie followed Kate, giving Emily a quick wave from his wrist. Sorcha trotted ahead of them. Geordie would find out about the hiding place tomorrow. Of course, it couldn't hurt if she looked around by herself.

She waited until they'd disappeared over the crest of the hill, then she strode to the house. She examined the front step, but it was still roped off. She decided it might not be dry enough for her to walk on. Instead, she used the plank at the back door.

Inside, though, it was almost completely dark, like the inside of a well with a lid on it, and Emily knew she wouldn't be able to see anything properly. She'd have to come back again during the day. She almost tripped on a small pile of rocks as she made her way back outside.

When she stepped outdoors, the stars glistened in the darkening sky and a soft breeze lessened the heat in the air. She could feel everything settling into silence, except for the faint hoot of an owl and the odd chirp of a cricket. Tiny scrabblings sounded in the grass a short distance across the yard.

Making her way back to the hole in the foundation, Emily manoeuvred herself into position and set the carved bird into its hiding space. But nothing happened. She stared down at the carving, then clutched it again in her hands. She shuffled about trying to find the exact spot she'd stood in when she came, but nothing worked. What did she have to do to get back home? Didn't she have to leave the carving behind? As the questions crowded into her mind, she set the bird inside the hole and bent to look inside. As she did so, she stretched her hand against the stone house to steady herself.

Suddenly, she was back home! Of course! She had to be touching the house at the same time as she placed the carving in the empty space – just as she had to touch the sentinel rock and Emma's special stone to move through time. She looked into the hole and saw the weathered carving perched inside. Yes, now she had a chance to do both things in the morning, to go to the wedding and watch the auction. She chuckled as she stepped out of the flowerbed and brushed herself off.

She found her mom and Aunt Liz at the kitchen table sorting through stacks of papers from a pile of filing boxes on the floor.

"Nothing yet," Kate looked up as Emily entered the room.

"I'm going up, then," Emily said.

"Would you like a snack before bed?" Aunt Liz asked.

Emily shook her head.

"You didn't eat much supper. You should probably have something. Besides, we're quitting now," Kate declared.

"We are?" Aunt Liz asked with a raised eyebrow. "You might be, little sister, but I'm not."

With hackles raised, Kate replied, "What's the point of carrying on? There's nothing here and you know it."

"I don't know it for sure, and neither do you."

Kate stood, putting her hands on her hips. "I've had enough for one night. We all need to get some rest for the big day tomorrow. I don't see anything that needs to be done that can't wait until tomorrow. The work will still be waiting for us."

"Since when are you in charge, Miss Bossy Boots?" Aunt Liz asked.

Kate spluttered. "I told you not to call me that!"

The little hairs on Emily's arm stood up. She felt like she was hearing an echo. How uncanny that her mom and Kate from the past were so similar.

Aunt Liz laughed. "Then quit acting like that!"

Chagrined, her mother said, "Sorry, I guess I do get carried away at times."

"Try *all* the time," Aunt Liz said sarcastically, but with amusement in her voice.

Kate put her head in her hands, "I just can't help it!"

"Don't we know it," Aunt Liz said, winking at Emily.

Emily breathed a sigh of relief. She'd never seen her

mom and aunt fight before and was glad their differences had ended so amicably.

Emily cleared her throat. "I think I'll just go to bed."

Aunt Liz held out her arms. Emily went over and gave her a hug. "Pleasant dreams, kiddo."

"Goodnight, Aunt Liz," Emily squeezed her tight.

"Do I get one too?" Kate asked, giving her a lost-puppy look.

"Sure, Mom," Emily went around and gave her a bear hug.

"Good night, sweet pea!" Kate said. Sweet pea was what her mom had called Emily when she was small. Maybe it reminded her of the time when their family had been happy together.

"Night."

Emily hesitated by the door. "Do you want me to take some of those papers up with me and see if I can find something?"

"No thanks," her mom said quickly. "We've got them all organized!"

Aunt Liz poked Kate in the arm. "You're doing it again!"

Kate smiled and shook her head. "Thanks anyway, Em, but you need your rest. We'll have plenty of time after the sale," she said more gently.

"Unless you really want some reading material," Aunt Liz said. "I came across this journal of your great-grandmother's that you might find interesting."

"Sure," Emily took the leather-bound journal with pleasure. It was one more connection to her past and to her ancestors.

As Emily headed upstairs, she savoured the familiarity of her grandmother's house, trying to remember how many times she'd gone up these same stairs. She found herself reminiscing about how the house used to be when her grandmother was alive, where the furniture sat, and all the knick-knacks and the pictures on the walls. Everything was blank now, except for the memories. And after tomorrow, there was no going back to the way the farm used to be.

Suddenly, she realized that the step near the top of the attic stairs hadn't squeaked as usual. Had she not stepped in the right place? She tested it again, putting her weight in different places. No more creaking. She recalled Geordie pounding the extra nails into the step. Was that why it was silent now?

Could she affect the present by what she did in the past? That could be scary! Nailing a step didn't seem too serious, but what if she altered their lives somehow?

She undressed slowly, considering the possibilities. After she pulled her nightgown over her head, Emily padded over to the trunk at the bottom of her bed and drew out her grandmother's "crazy" quilt. There were pieces of clothing sewn into it from all of her grandmother's family, all the people that Emily knew from pioneer times. She found a chunk of Geordie's shirt and a swatch of Emma's blue flowered dress.

Everything kept changing in her life — in the past and in the present. She'd had no idea at Easter time that her parents would be splitting up. And returning to the past, she found great changes had taken place with Emma's family too.

Crawling under her covers, she drew her grandmother's quilt over her and picked up her great-grandmother's journal. She read, "Margaret Elsbeth" on the inside front cover. The diary began three years after they'd moved to Canada on July 13, 1903. Emily skimmed the pages and laughed when she came to an entry that read, *"Today Kate dropped the cream jug and tried to blame it on Beth. Fortunately, we can still use it, as the handle and spout are intact."*

Emily continued reading here and there until she came to August 29, 1903. *"A beautiful day for my dear son's wedding..."* She stopped herself from reading more. She wanted to see the wedding for herself. She jumped backwards a few pages and began reading again.

She was almost mesmerized to sleep, reading all the entries about weather, purchasing stock, gardening, preserving, and general activities they did in their daily lives, just to exist. Finally, she gave up trying to keep her eyes open and set the diary on her nightstand, switching off the light with a contented yawn.

CHAPTER TEN

B *RIIIIING.*
Emily sat up. Her heart racing, she stared ahead in a daze. Then she thumped her alarm clock, and flopped back down. *5:30 a.m.* She groaned, then swung her feet out of bed and tiptoed to her clothes. She moved quietly, fumbling as she dressed, still not quite awake, but determined to see Geordie first thing.

Even though she knew the step didn't squeak anymore, she avoided it, just in case. Her mom's bedroom door was closed tightly as she passed by, but Aunt Liz's was open a crack. Emily slid by and made it to the kitchen without any problem – and came to a dead halt. Aunt Liz was making coffee at the counter.

Her aunt started, "Sheesh, you scared me, Emily."

"Sorry, Aunt Liz." Emily inched to the back door and set down the sneakers she'd been carrying.

"What are you doing up so early? Not able to sleep?"

"Not really," Emily admitted. "I thought I'd go out for some air."

"How about we go together?" Aunt Liz suggested.

Darn, thought Emily. How would she ever get away? She couldn't say no to her aunt without seeming rude.

"Sure," Emily said lightly.

"I'll be with you in a jiffy," Aunt Liz poured herself a cup of the fresh brew.

Emily sat on the step in the quiet of early dawn and gazed out across the peaceful farmyard and the pastures beyond. Sparrows flitted back and forth across the yard, and canaries and goldfinches twittered in the caraganas at the side of the house. After the auction, she and her mom would only be here for two more days, before they closed up the house and left for an indefinite time. She breathed deeply, trying to absorb as much as possible of her serene surroundings to remember later.

Aunt Liz touched her shoulder and handed her a glass of orange juice as she sat beside her. Together they looked out over the landscape in silence. A hawk soared overhead, then dived into a nearby field. The air smelled fresh and clean, although it was already warming with the rising sun, promising to be another scorcher of a day.

Emily stirred from the interlude. Since there was no chance for her to go into the past, she might as well start to unload the boxes of household goods that rested under the tarps, on the tables in front of the house. She sauntered over to one end. Aunt Liz followed, and they worked silently, setting out toasters, electric frying pans, sets of dishes, meat grinders, and huge roasters. Once they finished the kitchen things, they worked on the pictures and frames and other decorative objects from the china cabinet and walls of the house. Linens and clothing came next.

Emily and her aunt said little as the tables came alive with the personal effects of the family. When they finished, they stood back and admired their work. Emily caught sight of her mother watching from the veranda and motioned her over.

Kate joined them, forming a row along the table: Kate, Emily, Aunt Liz. The three of them instinctively put their arms around each other's waists and surveyed the scene. Several moments later, they heard the sound of a tractor in the distance. All at once, the morning became active with the cawing of crows and the crowing of a rooster somewhere in the distance. A cow bellowed and they could hear the faint tinkle of its bell.

"Ready for breakfast?" Aunt Liz broke the contemplative mood. "I'm making pancakes."

"Mmm, great!" Emily could already taste her aunt's mouth-watering whole wheat-blueberry pancakes. She served them with plain yogourt and chokecherry syrup. They were the best Emily had ever eaten.

"I'll set the table," she offered, heading for the house.

They left Kate outside, wandering down the row of tables. Emily saw her from the window, fingering objects, moving them slightly, lining them up a little more squarely. By the time she finished, everything was in neat rows. Emily motioned Aunt Liz to come and see. When her mom came into the house, Emily and Aunt Liz laughed at her.

"What?" she asked innocently, knowing very well what they found so funny.

By the time they'd eaten and tidied up the kitchen, the auctioneer's truck was pulling into the driveway. Two men got out and began setting up the sound system and the table where buyers would sign up for their numbered paddles and make their payments.

Shortly afterwards, the women from the local community group arrived. Agnes Barkley, wearing a baggy flowered tent dress, was among the first to poke her head inside. She gathered Emily into a huge, billowing hug that left them both gasping for breath. The kitchen grew crowded as the ladies began preparing big urns of coffee and arranging the lunch area in the veranda. They bustled in and out for water and utensils and cutting boards. They unloaded assorted sandwiches from plastic containers, along with home-baked tarts and squares and a few pies. One of the women started water boiling for hot dogs, even though it was too early to serve them.

Emily and her aunt carried out all the condiments, the plastic cups, stir sticks and other necessary gear. At the last minute, Kate decided there should be places for people to sit, and whisked out to the garage and brought back stacks of lawn chairs, which she set in the shade beside the house and on the veranda. When the coffee was ready, Emily carried two Styrofoam cups filled with coffee out to the auctioneers. Gerald and Donald came to get their own.

Just as Emily felt there was a lull with nothing left to do but wait, the first vehicles pulled into the yard. Before she knew it, the parking area filled up and the overflow lined both sides of the road, with the rest directed to a designated area in the pasture. Just like being at the town fair, except more compact, Emily thought. The only things missing were horse racing and bingo.

Emily meandered through the crowd, greeting neighbours. Soon everyone gathered in front of the long tables, where Pete Steinbeck, the jaunty auctioneer, began his spiel through a megaphone. Emily couldn't keep up with his fast-paced talk, but obviously others could, and soon the bidding began. She watched for a good half-hour, caught up in the excitement, then realized with a jolt that she needed to get to Geordie's if she was going make it to the wedding. The sun was already higher than she expected.

Strolling up to the house, she saw her mom and aunt sipping coffee on the porch steps. Everything seemed under control, although Agnes Barkley eyed her movements with interest.

Nonchalantly, Emily lost herself in the crowd surrounding the tables, until she was certain Mrs. Barkley couldn't see her. She edged away, while everyone's focus was on the bidding. Slipping around the corner of the house, Emily quickly reached the secret spot. Her hand on the wall, she felt inside the hole and took out the carving.

Instantly, she felt herself flung into the past. The sun hadn't quite reached the highest point in the sky, so Emily knew she hadn't missed going to the wedding. Not a sound came from within the stone house or the surrounding yard. Of course, she thought, they didn't live here yet. She hurried to the old homestead site. As she ran, Emily pulled a cloth-covered elastic out of her pocket and tied her hair back to keep it from flying into her face.

Even before she reached the sod house, she could hear the pandemonium. The family called to one another as they harnessed two chestnut Clydesdale draft horses and hooked them up to the farm wagon. They walked them over to the shed. From the side of the building, George Sr., Sandy, and Jack carried planks and sawhorses, loading them easily into the back of the wagon. Then they continued to the house.

There the girls and their mom chatted as they carried crocks and bowls of food to the wagon. Duncan and Geordie loaded them tightly against the back of the seat, making sure they wouldn't move on the journey. Geordie unloaded the last of the firewood inside the house, dodging the girls' procession.

Emily watched from behind a stand of poplars next to the house. Geordie hadn't spotted her yet. She didn't know how to get his attention without distracting him. Then to her dismay, as if on some hidden cue, the family scrambled into the wagon. Geordie's parents sat on the front seat with Molly squeezed between them. All the others scrambled into the back of the wagon and sat on the boards placed like benches along the sides. Geordie hopped onto the end with his legs dangling over the end. Sorcha tried to hop on board too.

"Stay, girl!" Geordie's dad commanded. Sorcha made a couple of circles in the middle of the road, and whined, but she stayed in the yard.

Emily waited for her chance. As the wagon creaked past her, she leapt onto the end beside Geordie. Startled, he grabbed for her, nearly letting her fall as she scrambled to get settled. The commotion caused everyone in the back of the buggy to turn around. Fortunately, Molly was tucked between her parents and couldn't see behind her.

"I wasn't hanging on proper," he called to them. "I'm fine now."

Emily clutched him, trying to right herself. Geordie grinned from ear to ear.

"I'm glad you made it in time," he whispered, his voice unnoticed under the chatter of the family and the rumbling of the wagon wheels.

"How far is it?" Emily whispered.

Geordie held up four fingers, indicating the number of miles.

They clopped along in a northwesterly direction, passing narrow dirt trails that wound across the pastures and led to small shacks and other homes. Geordie mumbled some of the names of the inhabitants. She caught some that she recognized, like Ferguson, McGuillvary, and Henderson, and others she didn't know, like Parley, Davidson, Vipond, and Campbell. The number of settlers in the Moffat area compared to the Glenavon district astounded Emily. There seemed to be one homestead right after another.

Emily stared at her surroundings in amazement. At least twenty-five rigs – wagons and carts – were parked along the trail and in the yard, most on the bald prairie, or under a few scraggly trees. The horses and oxen had been unhitched and led to a fenced area in a meadow where they grazed on short grass, or stood in the shade of a grove of poplars and chokecherry bushes. Some men had arrived by horseback, dismounting and joining the jovial crowd. The Elliotts alighted from their wagon amid cheery greetings from those arriving nearby.

Emily jumped off the wagon and moved away from the family, as they gathered the food they had brought. Geordie accepted a pie handed to him and motioned Emily to follow him up the curved dirt lane. They kept their distance from the family as much as possible without it seeming odd that Geordie wasn't joining in the festive behaviour. Molly acknowledged Emily with a smile and a little wave, but skipped ahead to join some other little girls.

In the yard, a small one-and-a-half-storeyed stone house stood before her with Virginia creeper crawling up its sides. The entrance to the back garden was through an arbour made of thin, stripped tree trunks and latticed branches. Although creeper grew on its sides, flowering sweet peas were also intermingled, and the whole thing decorated with colourful ribbons.

Emily stood with her back against some caragana bushes and watched everyone mingling and chatting. Then suddenly, there was a hush as the door opened and the minister strode into the yard. As he took his place near the arbour, the guests positioned themselves for good viewing.

Moments later, Sandy appeared with a huge grin on his face. He and his best man, his older brother Jack, joined the staid Presbyterian minister to his left. A lovely voice began singing and a delighted Molly traipsed from around the side of the house, strewing her path with fresh wild rose petals from a small willow basket. Behind her, a young woman appeared, holding a small bouquet of cut flowers, followed by the bride in a floor-length cream-coloured silk voile dress, with a wreath of multi-coloured blossoms adorning her head. She held a bouquet of sweet peas and ferns, and smiled demurely as she came to stand beside the grinning groom.

The guests stood patiently listening to the traditional words. Emily found herself fascinated, just looking at all the old-fashioned outfits. The men wore shirts, ties, and waistcoats, and some held soft felt hats or straw ones in their hands as they stood respectfully listening. The women, in their long dresses with leg-of-mutton sleeves and turned-down lace collars, did not wear any hats, which surprised Emily.

When the final words ended and the bride and groom sealed their ceremony with a kiss, the minister led the bridal party back inside the house to sign the necessary documents. They returned a few moments later through the arbour, and stood just inside the yard.

The minister announced, "I present Mr. and Mrs. Alexander Elliott."

The crowd pressed forward with words of congratulations. A small man appeared at the back of the crowd with a big black camera on a wooden tripod. He set it up near the entrance of the house and pointed it at a large area in front of some trees. Once he had inserted the glass plate, and drawn the black cloth over the back of the camera, he began gathering everyone for a photograph.

Emily watched from the corner of the house. It seemed to take longer to line up the forty people for the photograph, than the whole ceremony had taken, but at last, they all were ready. As the photo was taken, Emily suddenly realized this was the one she'd found in her grandmother's attic in the spring. She shivered at the thought of actually being present for the taking of that photo.

After the group photograph, the crowd dispersed, leaving only the wedding party, and then finally just the bride and groom to have their shots taken. Meanwhile, several men set up plank tables with crude sawhorses for legs. Subdued chatting continued as everyone took their places at the long benches and tables. Some children and bachelors sat on the mowed grass. Emily was amazed when several ladies brought a hearty soup out of the kitchen and served everyone.

Soon afterwards, the aromas of rabbit stew, roast chicken, meat pie, and cold ham filled the air. Emily watched as these foods were passed from one to another, along with potatoes, cooked carrots, and creamed peas. Hard-cooked eggs, sliced cucumbers and tomatoes, cheese, and other delicious side dishes followed. Once these were consumed, the women brought out oatcakes, Scotch shortbread cookies, scones, wild raspberry jam, saskatoon pies, and other fancy baking.

There were many speeches and toasts and finally the married couple cut the wedding cake – heavy fruitcake full of currants and peels. Not long afterwards, the minister left, and then the wedding guests lightened up and the merriment began with fiddle music and dancing.

Emily knew she had to go long before the Elliotts would be ready to leave. The little problem of how to manage it niggled at her now. She was at least four miles away from the sentinel rock, and even further from the stone house. How was she going to return home?

CHAPTER ELEVEN

Geordie seemed to sense her dilemma. He excused himself from the happy throng with a smiling nod and motioned for her to follow him out of the yard. Emily ducked between some trees and met him near the meadow where the horses browsed.

"What are we doing?" Emily asked.

"Going to get you home," Geordie turned his smiling freckled face to her.

"Won't they notice you're gone?"

"I won't be gone long!" He shook his head. "Have you ever ridden a horse before?"

"Once or twice," Emily said, staying where she was. The huge muscular Percherons, Clydesdales, and other large draft horses intimidated her by their sheer size.

"But we're four miles away from the sod house. You'd be gone a long time."

"Not cross-country," he said, slipping under the fence.

"It'll take too long to saddle up," she said. She looked around for saddles, but didn't see any. Geordie was petting one of their Clydesdales.

"We don't need to," he laughed.

"We're going bareback?" Emily gulped. She preferred something to hang onto. It at least gave her the illusion of being safe. "I've never done that before."

"Guess, this will be your first time, then!" Geordie laughed. "Come on, I'll get you back, but we'll have to be quick."

Emily climbed under the fence, and moved close to Geordie. She stared up at one of the Elliotts' immense Clydesdale horses, standing like a solid brick wall in front of her. She was only half its height. She swallowed hard.

"Uh, I don't think I can get up on it." She stepped back, suddenly feeling overwhelmed.

"Sure you can," said Geordie. He led the animal to a large boulder. Standing on the rock, he mounted, then held out his hand to Emily.

Knowing there wasn't any choice, Emily grabbed Geordie's hand and pulled herself up on the rock. Still holding his hand for support, she managed to get her leg over the horse's broad back and mount behind Geordie.

They swayed and the horse did a little dance. She was sure they were gong to topple over.

"Whoa, Betsy," he spoke to the horse quietly.

"What if we both fall off?" Emily quavered.

"We won't. I promise."

Emily nodded, not taking her eyes off the huge beast beneath her.

"Hang on tight, lass!"

"I will," she all but whispered into his back.

"Ready?" he asked Emily.

"Yes."

Geordie leaned over the horse's neck and grasped the coarse mane with both his hands. Emily leaned with him, staying as tight to him as she could, with her arms wrapped around him in a tight bear hug. As he dug his heels into the horse's side, Emily closed her eyes. They were off.

After a while, Emily glanced at her surroundings. Wisps of trees and clouds sped by as they cantered along. She clenched her teeth to keep them from rattling in her head.

"You don't have to hold onto me so tightly," Geordie called back to her. "I'd like to be able to breathe!"

She loosened her fingers from their white-knuckle grip, but kept her arms clasped around his thin body. She never relaxed the whole time.

When they arrived at the stone house, she slid off the horse gratefully and almost collapsed on the ground. Geordie laughed at her. She straightened herself up, pushing her hair away from her face. Somewhere along the way, she'd lost her hairband.

"The wedding was fabulous!" Emily said. "And thanks for getting me back!"

"I'm happy you enjoyed yourself, lass," he said. "Come again, when you can!"

"I will," she called up to him.

He saluted her. Then he spun the horse around and headed back across the pasture at a trot, his red hair flying back against the wind.

When she'd straightened up, Emily sprinted for the stone house. She eyed the back door, her mind whirring with the possibility of going inside. She wouldn't really be breaking and entering. She lived there, after all. She just wanted a quick peek to see if they'd done more work on the fireplace.

Cautiously, she mounted the plank stairway and opened the door. On tiptoes, as if afraid to disturb anyone or anything, she made her way into the parlour. She dropped to her knees in front of the unfinished fireplace and studied the construction. The stone chimney was partially finished and the hearth was all but done. She saw the rock that needed to come out to reveal the hiding place, but it took some time to figure out how the contraption worked to move it. At last, she rested on her heels and smiled. She knew the answer. No time to lose. She had to return home!

She slipped outside and made sure to close the door properly. She knelt at the house foundation. Without hesitation, she placed the carving into its hole and found herself crouched in the flower bed behind her grand-mother's house.

Agnes Barkley stood above her, shrieking.

Although dazed, Emily jumped to her feet.

"What's wrong?" she yelped. "What's happened?"

She took a quick look around. There were just the two of them. And neither of them was bleeding as far as she could tell. By then, some of the nearby auction-goers rushed around the side of the house. Among them was Emily's mom.

"What's all the commotion?" Kate asked, going first to Agnes Barkley's side.

Mrs. Barkley shook from head to toe and her jowls wagged as she pointed speechlessly at Emily. Kate turned to Emily.

"What's wrong? Is someone hurt?" She turned back to the still-shaking woman. "Mrs. Barkley, are you okay? Can you talk?"

Aunt Liz appeared with a glass of water and handed it to Mrs. Barkley, who downed it in one solid gulp that left her gasping. A few people stayed, but most of the small crowd disappeared again when they didn't see anything amiss.

"You!" Mrs. Barkley shrieked, pointing at Emily. "You just appeared out of the air and dropped at my feet!"

"And you scared the living daylights out of me," rebuked Emily, trying to prepare a plausible explanation.

"Come now, Agnes," Eunice Henderson, one of the other ladies, patted her on the back. "You know that's not possible."

"But she did," Mrs. Barkley insisted, her double chins trembling with emotion.

"Emily, what did you do?" her mom demanded.

"Fell into the flower bed," Emily said, as truthfully as she could manage.

Aunt Liz looked from Emily to the flower bed to the step and back again. She had a queer look on her face, but she said nothing.

"What were you doing back here, anyway?" asked her mom.

"Just taking a break."

Her mom eyed her suspiciously. "We'll discuss this later," she said. "Now, apologize for scaring Mrs. Barkley."

"Me scaring her!" Emily muttered to herself, but then she caught sight of the glare in her mom's eyes. She apologized contritely.

One of the other ladies, Eunice Henderson, guided Agnes Barkley back to the front of the house.

"I'll get to the bottom of this," Kate warned Emily.

Aunt Liz interrupted. "I wouldn't worry about it too much," she said. "Agnes will get over it. You know how she's always reading things into situations that aren't really there."

"I suppose," answered Kate. "Guess we'd better get back and see how things are going."

Emily followed the others back into the main yard. The crowd had thinned considerably and the auctioneers had moved their gear to the row of implements. The women mostly sat around the front step, sipping cool lemonade as they waited for their husbands to bid on the farm equipment. The yard was almost empty now that all the smaller goods had sold. Some people had paid for their purchases and left, while others would come back later or even the next day to haul the bigger stuff away.

Mrs. Barkley sat in the shade on the veranda, fanning herself, her eyes closed. Emily crept past her and sauntered into the kitchen, which was cluttered with empty plastic bins, bowls, pans, and utensils. Empty cardboard boxes and garbage bags full of used paper plates and glasses littered the floor. Emily groaned when she saw the sink heaped with dishes.

Searching around in the fridge, she found a leftover chunk of cheese, and munched on it as she watched the scene through the window. The community women cleaned off the tables and cleared out the veranda, trotting back and forth into the house. Emily knew there was no point in touching the fireplace until everyone had gone. She sat down at the table and glanced at the local newspaper, paging through it absent-mindedly.

Mrs. Henderson offered her a plate of leftover sandwiches and goodies, but Emily declined. She accepted a tall glass of lemonade, though, thinking about the wedding she'd just attended. They'd been drinking some kind of sparkly raspberry punch. Then she remembered the wedding photo. She had the original in her room.

Dashing up the stairs two at a time, Emily got to her room and rummaged around in the trunk until she located the group photo. The sepia-toned print clearly showed the smiling newlyweds and their many family members and friends, just as Emily had seen them not long before. She flipped over the print and looked at the writing on the back – *Alexander and Susannah Elliott, 1900*. The date wasn't right. She'd been back in the past attending the wedding in 1903. She looked closer and noticed the last digit was faint and it was really a three. Satisfied, Emily wrote the date darker, before she returned the print to the trunk.

What seemed like hours later, they finally had the house back to themselves, and Emily made her way to the kitchen. Aunt Liz sank into a chair at the table. She waved away a cup of coffee that Kate offered her.

"I've had enough today to sink a battleship, as they say!"

"I think it's 'float' a battleship," Kate said.

Aunt Liz poked at her. "Whatever." She sighed.

Emily laughed as she sat down beside her, sipping a bottle of water.

"Everything went well!" Kate said, pulling out another chair.

"I'm amazed at what some people pay for junk!" Aunt Liz remarked.

"At least, we got rid of it all." Kate smiled.

"I'm bushed," said Aunt Liz. "How about we just have some poached eggs and toast for supper?"

"Sounds great. I couldn't face another sandwich or hot dog," Kate sighed.

After they'd eaten and talked over the day, Emily sidled out of the kitchen. Moments later, she stood in front of the fireplace, studying the configuration of the stones. Remembering what she'd seen in the past, she wiggled several until the large stone at the base clicked. She dropped on her hands and knees, and wrenched the stone free.

"Mom, Aunt Liz! Come here!"

"What on earth?" her mom, exclaimed, from the doorway.

Aunt Liz swept by Kate and they both joined Emily, staring at the gaping hole at the bottom of the fireplace.

"How did you figure it out?" her mom asked.

"She obviously has more patience than we do!" Aunt Liz said. "Well, go ahead, see what's inside."

Emily felt inside the dark crevice. Her fingers touched something heavy and square. The secret box, she thought, reaching in to pull it out. But when she had the object in the light, she found instead a large, black, leather-bound book.

"The family Bible!" Aunt Liz took it from Emily. "I wondered why we never found one."

"Is there anything else?" Kate asked.

Emily peered inside and felt around some more, but all she came out with was mortar dust.

"I'll get a flashlight," Aunt Liz handed the Bible to Kate and rose to her feet.

Moments later, they were all trying to peer inside.

"Nope, it's empty," Emily declared, deflated. "Then where's the box?"

"Maybe it doesn't exist anymore," her mom said, giving her a little hug.

Emily shook her head. "I don't believe that!" Perhaps she could learn more if she went back to the past one more time.

"This is pretty exciting anyway," Aunt Liz said, indicating the Bible.

They returned to the well-lit kitchen and gently turned the pages. They found the family information on pages in the centre of the book. The entire Elliott family was listed, even farther back than Emily had expected.

"Do you know how valuable this is?" Kate asked.

"Priceless," Aunt Liz answered with a hint of a smile.

"We can trace our family back to the late 1700s." Emily was thrilled.

She could draw up a family history chart and maybe even connect some of the old photographs to the people named. Even more reason for wanting to keep her grandmother's stone house. There was just too much history embedded in it, right from the land and the building of the house, to the family living in it so many years, and all the memories it held in its walls and in Emily's heart.

"We just have to keep this house," Emily spoke determinedly. "There's too much of us here!"

"I agree that it will be hard to leave it, Emily," her mom said, "but you know the reasons why we have to let it go."

The phone ringing made them all jump. Her mom hurried to answer it. Obviously, she didn't want to talk about the house anymore. Emily listened for a few seconds, hoping it might be her dad, but she could tell it wasn't by the gentle way her mom spoke. Aunt Liz poured another cup of coffee and headed outside. Her mom finished the call and drifted out after her.

"That was Donald," she heard her mom say, "He was wondering if we needed a hand tomorrow. We just have to call him, if we do."

Aunt Liz laughed, "Someone has an admirer!"

"I don't think that's it," Kate responded. "He's just at loose ends right now."

"Well, we'll see if you're right."

Emily returned to the living room to examine the fireplace some more. As she got down on her knees on the floor, and pulled the stone out, she heard an odd scrabbling knock.

"Mom? Aunt Liz?"

She went into the hallway, but she could still hear them chattering outside. She returned to the fireplace to replace the stone. Something sounded again, but this time she heard definite knocking. She rose and entered the hallway again. Then she realized it was coming from the back door.

She walked to the door and put her ear against it. She jumped suddenly when the knocking came again. Were her mom and aunt playing tricks on her? She flung open the door.

"Geordie!" she gasped.

CHAPTER TWELVE

Emily stood there with her mouth hanging open.

"Aren't you going to invite me in, lass?" Geordie said with a smile that lit up his freckled face.

"How did you get here?" Emily stepped back for him to enter.

"I didn't exactly do it on purpose," he answered, looking about in bewilderment as he joined her in the hallway. He held out her hair elastic. "I found this on the ground in the yard."

Emily chuckled softly. "At least we know you can visit me, now."

"Now that I am here, will you give me a tour?" Geordie asked, looking curiously towards the kitchen.

Emily glanced furtively down the hall.

"My mom and aunt are outside, so we'll have to watch for them," she warned.

Geordie nodded, staring into each of the rooms as they came to them.

"It's the same, but so different," he said in awe, standing beside her in the dining room. "We never had a table like this."

"You will," said Emily. "My grandmother said her parents had it shipped over from Scotland."

Geordie shook his head. "I can't believe what the house is like now."

They moved into the small room that served as an office space and which held her grandmother's desk. Emily knew it was a bedroom in Geordie's home. Emily flipped on the light switch so he could see it better.

Startled, Geordie grunted in astonishment. "How did you do that?"

"It's electricity. There are wires running throughout the house. They bring power for lights and other things," she tried to explain.

"Where does this power come from?" His eyes were wide with wonder.

As Emily struggled to make him understand, she peeked out the window and saw her mom and aunt strolling across the yard away from the house. They were almost to the barn.

"Everything runs on power. Come, I'll show you."

Emily led him into the kitchen where she gave him a tour of all the kitchen appliances. Opening the fridge freezer, she had him stick his hand inside.

"It's like an icebox!"

"And this," she said turning on a burner, "is the stove. But don't touch it!"

She whirled through the kitchen demonstrating the toaster, the microwave and the coffee grinder. A clamour of noise erupted as everything popped, dinged, and ground. Geordie put his hands over his ears in fright.

Suddenly, the door burst open.

"What are you doing, Emily!" shouted her mom above the din. Aunt Liz followed behind her, staring about in astonishment.

Emily dashed around the kitchen turning everything off. "Just checking to make sure everything is working."

"I'd say it is!" Aunt Liz exclaimed.

Emily came to a standstill by the fridge in the abrupt silence. Geordie had backed himself between it and the door, and was edging himself behind it. He bumped into the broom hanging from the wall. Suddenly, it and the dustpan fell over with a clatter, and everyone jumped. Aunt Liz and her mom looked spooked.

"What caused that?" Kate looked suspiciously over at Emily.

She shrugged her shoulders.

"Now the place is haunted!" said Aunt Liz with a tense laugh

Emily heard Geordie stifle a giggle. She couldn't help smiling.

"Possessed is more like it!" Kate said with a touch of annoyance.

Geordie extracted himself from the mess and headed down the hallway, while Emily wondered how she could explain the situation to them. They obviously couldn't see Geordie, which was a good thing. She'd never be able to explain his presence.

All of a sudden, the light in the living room went on and off in rapid succession. Aunt Liz went to inspect, but Emily beat her there. She caught Geordie's hand as he was about to flip the switch again. She shook her head at him and pretended to be examining the connection.

"Just loose, I think," she said.

Nervously, Aunt Liz agreed.

"There certainly are a lot of peculiar things going on around here," Kate looked cautiously about.

"You know what these old places are like." Emily shrugged with as much innocence as she muster.

"A good reason for us not to bother with it any-more," Kate declared.

"Aw, Mom, just because a few things are a little unusual doesn't mean we shouldn't try to keep the place."

Geordie listened anxiously, obviously wanting to speak to Emily. She flicked the light off and left the room, hoping her mom and aunt would follow. They did.

"Guess I'll go up now to read," Emily said casually.

Behind her back, she motioned for Geordie to come with her. He waited until Kate and Aunt Liz returned to the kitchen, then crept up the stairs. As he entered Emily's bedroom and surveyed the contents, he hesitated.

"It's not seemly for me to be here," he said, his face turning crimson.

"Don't worry about it," she said. "Come, take a look."

She led him over to the open window. Geordie caught his breath at the sight.

"Look at how much those vines have grown – all up the side of the house and around this window, too. My mum would love to see this."

"Your mom planted the Virginia creeper? I didn't know it was that old."

Emily stared down at the lush, thick greenery, clinging to the walls and the old lattice, with a mixture of sturdy tendrils and woody stocks that clambered over the roof.

"What are those bushes down below?"

"Lilacs. My gran planted them when she was a young bride," Emily explained.

"There are other bushes and trees in the yard that we don't have back at home," said Geordie.

"I'm sure lots of things changed over the years," Emily said almost wistfully.

"It's so different," he said. "Now I understand how you feel when you visit me, lass."

He studied the fenced properties, and the patchwork of fields and pasture, noting where the roads ran. In the dusk, he could see the beginnings of the lights twinkling from the farmyards in the area.

"There are hardly any homes left now," he said sadly.

"The farms got bigger and many young people have moved away," she explained.

Then to change the topic, she asked, "So when did the wedding end?"

"Many stayed until dark," he answered.

"Did you get into trouble for taking the horse? Or did they even notice you were gone?" Emily quizzed him.

He chuckled. "Kate saw me return, but she didn't say anything, though I must keep on her good side so she won't tell on me sometime down the road."

"Where will the newlyweds live?" Emily asked.

"With Susannah's folks until we move into our stone house. Then she and Sandy will be living in our soddy until they have something built. He just took out his own homestead to the west of here."

He backed away from the window and looked at her room. His eyes came across the papers lying on Emily's nightstand.

Emily noticed his curiosity and said, "Speaking of homesteads, here are the papers from your parents' place." She picked them up. "They mention all the land that's broken and how many buildings and how big they are."

Geordie took them and began reading the first page.

"You can read?" Emily asked.

"Of course," Geordie said, amused. "I've been reading since I was Molly's age."

"But you don't go to school."

"Not right now, but I will be again once there's one built. In the meantime, my mum teaches us." He gave her a smile. "The Presbyterian church makes sure every child knows how to read from the Bible."

"I'm glad to hear education is important in your world," Emily said.

"Aye, there are several schools already in the Moffat area, but we're just a little too far from them to go every day."

They talked for a few minutes until Geordie noticed it was getting dark out.

"I think I'd better get back now." He headed for the door and flung it open.

Emily grabbed his shoulder. "Shhh. I have to get you out somehow, but without making my mom and aunt suspicious."

They could hear the two women's voices below. They were still in the kitchen and they'd be able to see Emily going to the back door. That wasn't such a smart idea at this point, she decided.

"You'll have to wait until they come up to bed."

"No, lass. I cannot," he said fretfully. "I've been gone too long and I don't know what will have happened."

He touched her softly on the shoulder. "Now I understand your concern."

"There must be another way." He strode over to the window and peered out again.

"It's too far down," Emily said in fear.

Geordie shook the old vine-covered lattice and it seemed secure.

"I'll climb down the creeper," he said, pushing himself onto the window ledge. "It's dark enough now no one will notice me against the house."

"I don't think the vines will hold. They're so old."

"I'll only fall into the lilac bushes," he said with a grin.

"That's too dangerous," she said.

"I will be fine, lass," Geordie patted her hand, and swung his legs over the edge. He held her hair tie in his hand and slipped it into his pocket. "Now I can come visit you when I have the time." He smiled and disappeared from sight.

Emily leaned over the window ledge and watched him climb down the Virginia creeper-covered lattice, amid rustling vines and creaking lattice. He managed to hang on until about halfway down when one of the fasteners came partially loose and he swung out from the house and came back with a thump against the wall. She watched as he steadied himself, then disappeared into the lilac trees. The next time she saw him was when he'd reached the ground and the glint of the moon caught his form. He gave a quick wave and stooped to place the hair tie in the space in the foundation. He disappeared immediately.

"Emily, are you okay?" She heard her mom pounding up the stairs.

"Fine, Mom," Emily called back, just as her mom burst through the door.

"There's someone outside. We think there might be a burglar!" Her mom panted. "Stay up here and bar the door," she ordered. "Aunt Liz and I are going to take a look."

Oh, no. They must have heard Geordie. What could she say? Emily stepped over to her mom.

"I'm sure everything is fine," she said.

"But we heard some rustling in the bushes outside and some kind of scraping or something. And then something hit the house."

Emily couldn't think of any logical way to explain what had happened.

"Didn't you hear it?" her mom asked with an incredulous look.

Emily shrugged her shoulders. "I guess I thought it was just the wind."

"Wind, my foot. There isn't a breath of air out there and you know it," Kate's face was getting redder by the minute.

"Well, I'm pretty high up here," said Emily, taking a step back. "I don't always hear what's going on down below."

Her mom looked as if she didn't believe a word. "Well, I don't know what's going on around here, but you aren't going anywhere from now on! You are not to leave this house. Do you understand?"

"Aw, Mom, that's not reasonable!"

"Reasonable or not, all I know is that ever since we got here and you've been traipsing out to that rock, curious things have been going on. You frightened poor Mrs. Barkley half to death..."

Emily held up a palm to stave off her mom's ranting. "She does it to herself."

"That may be, but there was more to what happened than you're letting on, I just know it," her mom declared. "Stay put while we go out to investigate."

Her mom left the room. Emily went over to the window and watched for her mom and aunt below. A few moments later, she saw them turn the corner of the house. They clung to one another as they poked around with flashlights. They examined the ground and the bushes, whispering as they went. It didn't take them long to find the broken branches in the bushes and the loose lattice.

Emily drew back from the window and plunked herself down on her bed. What possible explanation could she come up with? The damage started below her window, so the obvious conclusion would be that she was involved somehow. Her mom blamed her for everything. Of course, she *was* involved this time.

What was even worse was that she was forbidden to leave the house. Emily thought again about the box. She'd have to go back again somehow and be more persistent with Geordie. Clearly, he was her only hope to find the secret hiding place. The real problem, though, was slipping away from her mom and aunt so she could get back to the past. How would she accomplish that?

CHAPTER THIRTEEN

Emily smiled as she slipped out of her clothes and into her soft nightgown. She'd figured out how to go back to the past without her mom knowing. The last thing she did before hopping into bed was to set the alarm for five in the morning. She hoped to get up long before her mom or aunt. With a bit of luck, they'd be too tired after the work of the auction to get up early.

Emily pulled her grandmother's quilt over her and settled down to sleep beneath its comforting warmth. A cool breeze wafted in her bedroom window. Although tired, she wiggled and fretted, unable to sleep long after she heard her mom and aunt go to bed. Her thoughts kept returning to the homestead papers. At last she switched on her lamp and took up the documents.

She read them carefully, amazed again at the details of land cleared, and the size and cost of all the buildings. She turned to another page and all of sudden saw the reason why no land was cleared in 1903. The Elliotts had had a prairie fire. Puzzled, Emily studied the paper. The information must be wrong, because she knew the family was perfectly fine. Then with sudden realization, she gasped. Maybe it hadn't happened yet! Did her great-grandmother have anything about it in her diary?

Yanking open her nightstand drawer, she grabbed the diary, flipping through the pages until she came to September in 1903. She scoured the spidery handwriting until she came across a passage that caused her to sit up straight.

"A prairie fire almost destroyed our home yesterday. The winds were strong and the area so dry and brittle. We've lost so much. Some of our neighbours fared even worse."

Emily scanned the next few pages, but didn't find any more information about the fire. What had the Elliotts lost? How much damage had the fire caused? What had happened to the family? The journal failed to mention anything more. There was a gap of several weeks afterwards, almost as if her great-grandmother was too disheartened to write of it. But Emily had seen no evidence of it while she was in the past. How could that be? She compared the entry to the homestead papers, but there was nothing more there either. Then she examined the diary again and saw the date of the fire. September first. Two days after Sandy's wedding! She tried to think about how much time would have passed in Geordie's world since her visit to the wedding. Had the two days already passed?

She had to warn them, if she wasn't already too late! She fumbled out of the bedclothes. There was no time to lose. She dressed quietly and quickly, listening for sounds within the house, but there were none. Outside, the wind had picked up, and through her window, she saw the dark overcast sky. She'd have difficulty seeing without the light of the moon to guide her. She'd need a flashlight.

Before she left her room, she hastily fluffed up her bedding to make it look like she was still sleeping, hoping her mom and aunt would think she was still there, if they happened to check on her. She crept down the staircase, her sneakers in her hand, making sure not to make a sound. She grabbed a bottle of water and a flashlight from a drawer and slipped them into her backpack, along with an apple. Then she tiptoed down the hallway and out the back door. The wind howled around her as she laced up her runners, and reached for the carved bird.

Moments later, she found herself leaning against the stone house in pioneer time. The sun beat down on her from high in the sky and the air was stifling, in sharp contrast to the cooler weather she'd left behind. For the first time, she noticed the dryness of the landscape, the dying grass of the pastureland, and the dull, faded green of the bushes and trees. Even the bare ground seemed parched. She took a swig of water then set off to look for Geordie and his family.

As she rounded the corner of the house, Emily found the Elliotts sitting in the shade of some trees a short distance away, having a noonday picnic. How could she get Geordie's attention? She tried to calm herself. Maybe she was there a day early and they had plenty of time to prepare.

She watched the family share thick slabs of home-made sliced bread with hard-boiled eggs and chunks of cheese, then wash their food down with water, finishing off with oatcakes and pincherry jam. They sat in circular fashion on rough logs and short stacks of lumber. At last, George Sr. took a final drink of water, set his tin cup down, rose to his feet and strode off towards the out-buildings.

As Emily kept an eye on Geordie's movements, she watched his mom and the girls clear away the meal, and the men disperse back to their work at the house. They skimmed past Emily as she stepped out of their way, except for Geordie. She'd lost sight of him. Soon after-wards, Emily could hear the pounding of hammers and the sound of lumber being moved about. She peeked inside and saw Jack and Duncan sheeting the dividing room walls on the main floor. They were almost fin-ished.

She caught a sudden dark movement out of the corner of her eye, causing her to turn around. Geordie drove past her in a small cart with two oxen, heading down a trail through the pasture. In a flash, Emily chased after him. At first he didn't notice her, but it didn't take her too long to catch up, as the oxen travelled so slowly.

"Wait," she called out breathlessly, coming up beside him.

Startled, he jerked on the reins, but the oxen took some time to respond.

"You sure can scare a fellow," he laughed as Emily caught up. "I guess you are paying me back for shocking you the other night."

"I didn't mean to," she said. "But I need to tell you something important."

He reached down and pulled her into the seat beside him.

"There's a prairie fire coming. Your family needs to prepare for it."

He chuckled and pointed across the landscape, as he flapped the reins to get the oxen moving again. "Look, lass, there's nothing out there."

All around them, the prairies stretched and rolled, with long bent grasses, yellowing and brittle from the heat of the sun, and dotted with small trees and bushes that had lost most of their leaves to the heat and the autumn cycle. Dust rose in whirling puffs behind the cart as they followed the dry dirt trail winding along the contours of the landscape.

"I know it doesn't look like it right now," she said, "but it could happen any time."

"That's always a danger," he answered. "But I won't be gone long and surely it can't happen for quite some time." Geordie peered up at the dazzling sky and wiped his forehead with his arm.

Emily was tempted to agree as she scoured the serene countryside. In the distance, she saw fields with ripening crops and small homestead sites where wooden shacks or sod shanties stood. Songbirds flitted overhead and startled gophers chattered. The rasping of the wheels on the hard ground almost lulled Emily into believing nothing was about to happen. She had to be right, though, and she needed to convince Geordie of their imminent danger.

As they plodded along, she found it hard to concentrate. Riding behind oxen was scorching hot, because their slow pace didn't create any kind of air movement, and the cart seemed to hit every bump and clump of grass on the trail. Emily wrinkled her nose in distaste as they passed a stagnant slough. But the acute stench brought her thoughts into sharp focus.

"How long has it been since Sandy's wedding?" she quizzed Geordie.

"Two days," he answered.

She thought about it for a moment. "It's going to happen today," she said with certainty.

She saw that Geordie couldn't decide whether to believe her or not.

"I read it in your homestead papers and in your mom's diary."

He looked uneasy. "You must be mistaken. There's not even any wind."

Emily persisted. "You must convince your family of the danger. And you have to do it right now!"

"But I need to go to the old place to get feed for the livestock," he said.

"That can wait."

Geordie explained patiently. "We ploughed a fire-guard around the yard in the spring."

"I don't think that's enough," Emily said, recalling the grim words in her great-grandmother's diary. "Your family needs to get better prepared."

As her words died away, the wind rose and lifted Geordie's hair. Spooked, he turned the oxen around and headed home. Somewhat relieved, Emily sat back quietly as they plodded back within sight of the Elliotts' stone house.

Geordie spoke at last. "You have our homestead papers and my mom's diary that she's still writing in. You know more about our future than we do."

"I don't know everything, Geordie. But I'm sure about the fire."

He pointed to the darkening sky to the west.

"A storm is brewing." He anxiously flipped the reins along the oxen's backs to spur them on. A sudden wind gust buffeted them.

"I've never seen anything come up that quickly," Emily commented. Then she noticed a band of dull red light in the distance.

Sudden fear gripped her. She touched Geordie on the shoulder. "It's not a storm."

The wind increased and the brightening crimson on the horizon spread and widened. The oxen sensed the changes. They moved faster now, but were harder to handle, twisting and jerking with each gust of wind. Suddenly, Geordie yanked the beasts to a stop. The oxen bellowed and jerked at their harness almost upsetting the buggy.

"Jump off," Geordie yelled, as he leapt from the swaying buggy and went to the front of the yoked pair.

Emily vaulted out of the buggy and ran to help Geordie calm the oxen. But as she came up the other side of them, she drew back, uncertain what the huge beasts would do. Swiftly, Geordie unharnessed the oxen, then slapped them on their rumps.

"What are you doing?" Emily asked anxiously.

"Freeing them to find their own shelter. It'll be faster if we run." They watched the animals head over a nearby hill.

He grabbed Emily's hand. "Come on. We have to warn the others."

As Emily and Geordie pounded across the prairie back to the stone house, the wind increased and so did the height and width of the band of red on the horizon.

Moments later, they were within shouting distance of the homestead. Emily could smell smoke now.

"Dad! Mum!" Geordie yelled as he ran. "Fire! Prairie fire!"

Emily felt herself falling further behind and Geordie sprinted faster. "You go on," she yelled at Geordie. "I'll catch up."

Family members emerged from the house, out-buildings, and garden, gathering around Geordie. In a moment, Jack and Duncan raced to round up and harness the horses, while George Sr. ran to the plough to help hook it up. The girls grabbed feed buckets and pails from all over the yard and ran towards the well, their hair and dresses flying in the wind. Geordie's mom raced to an outbuilding and came out with an armload of gunnysacks.

A thick front of smoke stretched from north to south as far as she could see. The older boys had harnessed the horses now. Jack drove one horse around the outskirts of the yard with the sixty-centimetre breaking plough, while Duncan with his horse hooked up to the disk harrows, went in the other direction. Both churned up the earth as fast as they could go, concentrating on the western side of the yard, before going around their whole farmyard, struggling to keep the frightened horses in line.

George Sr. loaded an empty water barrel onto the stoneboat, and he and Geordie dragged it to the well with all the strength they could muster. Bella and Beth soaked the gunnysacks in the water trough as fast as Geordie's dad could pump more water into it. Then Geordie filled the water barrels in tandem with his dad for later use, while the girls ran the sopping sacks to the edge of their property. Kate and her mom ran about shutting the chickens in the henhouse and making sure the pigs were secure in their pen. Then they raced back to the well site to help some more. All at once, Geordie's mom looked around herself in some urgency.

"Molly," she called. "Where are you?"

She ran to the house. "Molly!" she screamed.

The other girls dropped what they were doing and began to search for her. Geordie and his dad joined the fray. Kate tore towards the garden running through the rows of tall corn, while her mom and Beth ran through the house. Geordie and his dad checked all the outbuildings. Emily ran too, checking around all the bluffs and stands of trees in the yard. She couldn't recall seeing Molly since she'd arrived. Everywhere she could hear people calling for Molly. George Sr. waved Duncan and Jack to continue breaking ground. There were already enough people searching for Molly, and the clouds of smoke were gaining ground.

Then as Emily rounded the caraganas, she came face to face with Geordie, sweating and breathing hard.

"We can't find Molly! She's always traipsing off by herself. I don't know where the wee bairn could be." His eyes filled with dread.

In a flash, it came to Emily.

"I do," she said, and took off at a full-tilt run across the yard.

Geordie quickly caught up to her and they kept pace as they stumbled over the newly-tilled ground, and then ran flat out across the prairie to a stand of poplars. As they drew close, they could hear Molly talking to her doll, placidly playing tea. Emily skidded to a stop to catch her breath, so she didn't frighten the little girl. She motioned to Geordie to do the same.

"Hello, Molly," Emily tried to keep the quaver out of her voice, as she pushed aside the branches.

She looked up in surprise. "Emily," she said. "And Geordie. Have you come for tea?"

"Not this time, Molly," Emily said gently. "We've come to take you home."

Molly frowned, "But I like it here."

"Come on, lassie," Geordie said. "Mum's looking for you. She wants to make sure you're safe."

Molly stared ahead, unseeing, as if listening to something inside her mind. She shook her head. "We cannae go home."

Geordie scooped her up.

"I can't leave Jane," she yelled.

Emily grabbed her doll and Molly pulled it close

as they pushed out of the bush. They came to an abrupt halt at the edge of the trees, watching the flames race across the dry prairie faster than a galloping horse, straight towards them. The towering wall of fire, at least a kilometre wide, burned everything in its path, igniting small bushes, and chasing small frenzied creatures as it rolled over the dry grass. In the distance, someone's shack burst into flames in the rising wind.

Within moments, the air around them filled with the smell of burning grass and bushes. Flocks of birds rose to the skies, squawking. Flames shot into the air from an overpowering cloud of bluish black smoke- between them and the stone house.

"What are we going to do?" Emily screamed.

"We'll never make it to the house!" Geordie yelled above the crackling of the fire. He swung Molly onto his shoulders. "We have to find someplace the fire can't reach us! A ploughed field or some water."

Emily watched the sheets of flame roll towards them, following the contours of the land, skirting a larger grove of trees that moments later ignited. Fear gripped her as fire leapt over the dirt trail about two kilometres or so behind them. She scouted around for a nearby field or one the stinky sloughs they'd passed earlier, but couldn't see anything. The horrendous roar grew louder.

"Come on!" Geordie grabbed her hand. "We'll make a run for it!"

"Wait!"

Emily snatched off her backpack, suddenly remembering what was in it.

"Leave it! There's no time for anything," Geordie shouted.

"I have water," she yelled back.

He nodded and pulled a cloth handkerchief out of his pocket. As Emily fumbled to open the bottle of water, Geordie shoved Molly's doll into the backpack. Together they wet the handkerchief, and Geordie handed it to Molly, instructing her to keep it over her face. Molly nodded, her eyes big and round with fright. Then he ripped off a portion of his shirt, tore it in two, and soaked the pieces for Emily and himself. Emily threw the bottle back into her pack and in a moment they were running hard, Geordie struggling to keep Molly secure on his back.

As they ran, the wind drove into their backs. Bits of ash and other debris swirled around them. Their eyes stung and their throats burned, even with the moist cloths protecting their mouths and noses. Rabbits, coyotes, and birds crossed their path, trying to outrun the fire. They joined a rutted trail and watched as a burning clump of tumbling mustard swept past them and started a fire on the other side. How were they ever going to escape?

CHAPTER FOURTEEN

Emily was stunned by the power and speed of the fire. Looking back, she saw long tongues of flame shoot six to nine metres ahead of the main wall of flame. Clumps of "prairie wool" took to the air and came down as torches to the grass, starting new fires.

All at once, they caught sight of the oxen, plunging forward at a speed Emily had never seen them reach before. Their heaving bodies bulldozed across the pastureland, trampling small bushes, and they bawled loudly as the wave of flames crackled and roared behind them. Prairie chickens and other ground fowl wailed to one another in distress, skirring and flying in bewilderment before the dazzling flames.

Suddenly, Geordie shouted, "Follow the oxen!"

Emily hesitated momentarily. When she glanced back, she saw the fire had already engulfed the clump of bushes they'd just passed.

"They'll find water!" Geordie shifted Molly's weight and pulled Emily on.

They sprinted up a hill and lurched over the crest, heading into a small gully. When they rounded a thicket of willows, they saw the oxen aiming for a small slough just beyond. Emily and Geordie, with Molly bouncing on his back, pelted behind them as fast as they could go. Sparks flew around them and they slapped at those landing on their clothes. Emily kept behind Geordie to make sure Molly was safe. The vigorous wind whipped the soaring flames even higher and the sky was dark with smoke.

At last they reached the safety of the slough, plunging into the stagnant water, splashing to make themselves as wet as possible. If there was an odour, Emily could no longer smell it. The inside of her nose felt raw from breathing smoke. They waded as deep and as far into the centre as they could, right next to where the oxen stood. Everywhere, fearful eyes stared at them from other creatures in the pond. Geordie let Molly slide down and get herself fully wet, then he picked her up again and held her in his arms. Tears streaked down her smoke-blackened face, but she didn't whimper or say a word, just clung to Geordie panda bear-style.

All at once, thick smoke enveloped them, and the tall slough grass caught fire, zooming fifteen metres into the air. Terrified, Emily took a deep breath and sank below the water, feeling Geordie do the same beside her, as he instructed Molly to take a deep breath and plunge below the surface. Emily struggled underwater, holding her breath and keeping the green slime from entering her mouth.

Each time she raised her head to gasp a breath of air, her lungs filled with smoke. She splashed wildly, trying to keep the flames away from herself. A terrible panic engulfed her as she thrashed about to keep herself low enough in the water, without getting her feet stuck in the mud at the bottom of the pond.

"I'm feart," Molly said, clinging to Geordie.

"We're all scared, little hen," he answered, hugging her tighter.

Emily willed herself to be brave and help Geordie keep Molly safe. She scooped water up and over the child, making sure her hair and back stayed wet.

Although it seemed like hours, only minutes had passed when Geordie signalled that it was safe to get out of the water. Debris and white ashes fluttered around them. Emily could hardly speak or breathe. She continued to hold the damp cloth to her mouth, which seemed to ease the pain. She took Molly from Geordie to give him a break.

Emily looked at Geordie. His eyes were red-rimmed and his face blackened by fire and smoke. His eyebrows were missing and his clothes were sopping wet, torn, and caked with mud and green slime. The oxen still bellowed and remained in the middle of the slough, bedraggled with soot and mud. Geordie made no move to retrieve them. He seemed to know that budging them would be like trying to move a stone wall.

The sky was still dark, and the grassland in the fire's wake was charred black, and desolate. All the ground covering was gone – from the grasses and weeds to the buffalo scrub, silver sage, and autumn flowers – everything was gone in one twist of natural fate. The wind howled around them and they could hear the crackling of the fire sweeping beyond them. The odour of burned grain filled the air.

Emily tried to stop her teeth from chattering. Geordie put his arm around her shoulder and held her close. Molly snuggled into her too, shivering. They held each other tight, trying to warm themselves up.

"We must get you both home," Geordie said. He trembled too.

"Where are we?" Emily inquired, her voice rasping.

"Not far," Geordie said. "Can you walk?"

She nodded. "I'll carry Molly for a bit."

"I can walk," Molly insisted, sliding to the ground and holding their hands tightly.

They headed to the east, around the other side of the bluff and the slough. This kept them at right angles to the fire. Molly quickly tired, and Geordie carried her in his arms. Soon, they came to the ridge of a hill. Emily could just make out the roof of the stone house in the distance. She smiled with relief and was about to say something to Molly, when she realized the child had fallen asleep.

All at once, the wind shifted. Geordie quickened his pace. The fire had changed direction – straight towards the Elliotts' home again, only on the other side. They began to run. Emily lagged behind, coughing and struggling for breath, while Geordie pummelled the ground in long frantic strides towards his family.

Emily came to a stop when a coughing fit wouldn't subside and signalled Geordie to continue without her. She retrieved her bottle of water and took huge gulps before soaking the handkerchief again and wiping at her eyes. Her heart thumped wildly as the fire exploded towards the farm. Her view suddenly became obscured. She could no longer see Geordie and Molly, or the stone house, beyond the wall of smoke. Securing her backpack once again, she hurried after them as fast as she could, but had to slow down when sudden pain stabbed her ankle. She must have twisted it, though she couldn't remember how or when. Every muscle in her body ached, and she had a pain in her side from running. She blotted at her eyes with the damp cloth and pressed onwards, watching the scene before her, helpless to do anything.

All she could do was pray that Geordie's family and their home would be all right. If only they'd managed to make a wide enough fireguard around their buildings. If they hadn't, she didn't want to think about their fate.

The stone shell of the house would still stand, but everything else could be destroyed.

When at last Emily neared the yard with the stone house, and the smoke cleared enough for her to see, she scoured the area for Geordie and Molly and the other family members. The fire had swept all around the buildings, leaving them surrounded by black earth. The yard looked like an oasis in the desert. But the garden was decimated and the corn patch reduced to blackened rubble.

Emily shed tears of joy when she saw the buildings intact, and couldn't stop a little scream when she saw Geordie emerge from a bluff with Molly in his arms. His parents ran to greet them.

"Not Molly too!" she heard Geordie's mom wail, fearing she had lost a second child. She sobbed with relief, realizing Molly was only sleeping, when she reached them. As she embraced the pair in one sweep, the little girl woke up and hugged her mother tight around her neck.

"Don't worry, Mum," she said, "I'm safe. Geordie and Emily saved me."

As she held her youngest daughter close, Geordie's mom looked out across the yard towards Emily and shivered. As she brushed Molly's tangled hair from her face, she said, "Thank heavens for your brother. And, well, whoever else saved you, I'm so thankful they did." Then she hugged Geordie tight to her again.

George Sr. patted him on the back. "You've done a man's job today!" he said. "I'm proud of you, lad!"

The others joined them then, coming from the south side of the house, along with Sorcha. They carried brooms, shovels, buckets, and wet sacks, sagging against one another as they stumbled across the yard. Smudged with ashes and smoke, their dishevelled appearance was a sight of beauty to Emily. All the Elliotts were safe.

Creeping closer, she could hear them talking about the frantic time they'd had putting out the sparks that jumped the cultivated circles around their home and ignited the dry grass close to the outbuildings. As their conversation died down, George Sr. and Jack walked the perimeter one last time, making sure all the sparks were out.

"Come Geordie," said his mom, "We need to get you and Molly into some warm, dry clothes."

She turned to the girls. "Kate, heat some water," she instructed. "I think we could all do with some good strong tea down us."

Emily thought then about the Elliott's sod house. All their personal belongings were there. She hurried over the burnt prairie towards their original farmyard, halting as she reached the edge of the burn's path. The soddy was just beyond it. She sighed with relief. The fire had changed direction before reaching their home. She turned back, watching Duncan mount one of the Clydesdales and head out across the land. Another rider, probably a neighbour, was silhouetted on a hill-side to the north. Emily watched as they met and stopped to converse. Then a third rider joined them from the direction of the sod house and she knew it was Sandy.

Emily headed back then. She noticed that Molly's bluff of poplars still stood and she smiled at the little girl's confidence in knowing she would have been safe at her special place. Emily arrived back in the yard as the others headed for the well to clean themselves off. Geordie had already washed and changed into clothes that looked like his older brothers'. She caught his attention. He ambled over to her and they slipped around the corner of the house.

"I'm so glad you and your family are okay!" Emily felt the tears sliding down her cheeks.

"Aye, lass, they are because of you!"

"I didn't do anything," Emily protested. "If only I'd come sooner! Maybe I could have helped save something."

"You warned me about the fire. And you helped save Molly!"

"And you gave back the stone and made me the carving," she said. "Without that I wouldn't be here."

"If I'd have listened sooner, maybe we could have saved more," He grimaced and kicked at a stone. "And if I hadn't been so stupid in the first place, stealing that stone, maybe Emma would be alive too!"

Stunned, Emily reached out to him. "Don't ever say that!" she said. "You know I couldn't have saved her. "

Geordie said nothing, as he looked out across the prairie.

"You don't believe me, do you?" Emily demanded.

He shrugged his shoulders.

"You must promise me you won't blame yourself. There's nothing any of us could have done!" Emily spoke softly, for the first time believing in her own heart that what she said was true.

"I miss her so much," Geordie whispered.

"I know. I do too," Emily said, pulling Geordie in for a hug.

He clung to her then for a few moments, then his body relaxed and he became calmer, as if his guilt was drifting away. Emily found her heart becoming peaceful too.

"It's been grand having you here," he said, stepping away. "Almost as if Emma were here."

Emily smiled. "Being with you helped me feel close to Emma again," she said.

"Our lives and our buildings are safe, at least here."

"Your other place is fine too," Emily told him what she'd seen.

"The garden's gone here, but Mum and the girls had most of it picked. We may still be able to dig up the root crops, if we can locate where they are."

"You'll do fine, Geordie," she said.

"That's right, lass. The main things are safe."

Just then, the other riders reached the yard. She and Geordie rushed over to hear what they had to say. They were thrilled to see that Sandy was safe.

Before he or Duncan could say a thing, the third young man started reporting his findings. "The Millars lost everything. The Fergusons' sod house is okay and the family is safe. They'd wet it down well, so the fire swept right over the top, but the sod didn't burn."

"Thank goodness they had enough sense to stay inside," Duncan added. "What about Susannah's family?"

"The fire didn't come that far west," Sandy said. "It missed us all completely, but I couldn't get through it to get here any sooner." He bowed his head. "I didn't know how any of you were faring. It's missed the soddy, too, thankfully, but so much of the land is destroyed."

"Yes, the fire was so hot in places, it burned deep into the roots of the prairie," said the young man. "The Davis's field of wheat stooks and their flax fields are burned to a crisp."

"Some of our crops are gone," Sandy said. "The last of our wheat and some of the oats."

George Sr. came up then and heard the last of what they said. "It'll be a tough winter for the animals, but we'll make it." His face was grim. "We'll have to band together to see what we can do for some of the folks who didn't fare as well as us."

The young man nodded. "Some are talking about meeting at the Moffat Kirk tomorrow evening."

"We'll be there," Geordie's dad said.

Duncan, Sandy, and Jack indicated they would be there too. The other rider nodded his assent, then continued on his way. Duncan and Sandy dismounted and the men gathered around them to hear more, but the women headed for the house. Geordie drew Emily to the side of the henhouse.

"I have to go back with Jack to get the oxen before they wander off."

"I must go too," she said. "I have no idea what is happening back at home, or what time it is." She looked down at herself, and chuckled. "Or how I will explain this."

Her clothes were tattered and grimy and her hair hung in straggly clumps. She imagined that her face was probably dark with soot and maybe even green slime.

"I'll never forget this day!" Geordie exclaimed.

"I won't either," Emily laughed.

"When will I see you again?" asked Geordie.

"I'm not sure," she answered. "My mom may never let me out of her sight again, especially when she sees how I look right now."

A well of sorrow rose inside her as she realized that she really might not see him again. She and her mom would be leaving the farm soon, and she had no idea when they'd be back. Suddenly, Geordie gave her a bear hug, as if knowing this might be the last time they'd meet.

As he stepped back, he said, "Come when you can, lass. You are always welcome...as a friend and a relative!"

Emily caught the sadness in his eyes. He strode back around the corner of the house.

"Wait," Emily called after him.

He stopped and came back.

"I need to know about the secret hiding place for the box."

He shook his head, amused. "I don't really know. All I do know is that my dad loves to hide secret drawers and compartments. He likes to challenge people, and hide things within things."

"But we've already found the spot at the bottom of the fireplace and the box wasn't there," Emily reminded him.

"I'm sorry, lass. Then I don't know," he said.

As Emily thought this through, Jack hollered for Geordie.

"Can't you give me any other hints?" Emily pleaded, knowing this might be her last opportunity.

"I can't think of anything. It must be something that he's not yet done."

"I suppose that could be it," Emily said, disappointed.

"If I do discover something, I'll let you know somehow." He smiled. "I'll write you a note!"

"Do you promise?" She smiled back at him.

"Aye, I do! Now, I must go, lass."

"Say goodbye to Molly for me."

He nodded and Emily watched him until he was nearly back with his family. Then he turned and gave her a salute. She waved goodbye, her throat aching from more than smoke.

As she straightened her backpack, she found Molly's doll. Where could she leave it for Molly to find again? As if in answer, the back door opened and two tired dark eyes peeked out at her. Molly stood there clean and tidy, in bare feet and wearing a fresh dress. She reached for Jane, and clasped her to her chest.

"Thank you for saving her, Emily. I knew you'd take care of her. You have a big heart."

Molly gave Emily a quick hug. Emily felt loving warmth surround them, and she knew that Molly – her gran – was going to be fine. Molly was surrounded by a family who doted on her and she was going to have a wonderful life, full of adventure and love.

As Molly disappeared back inside the house, Emily realized that just as Molly's growing up was natural and right, Gran Renfrew's death was also a natural occurrence. She had lived life to the fullest, with splendid people around her, in a place that she loved. In another flash of knowing, Emily understood that if Emma had grown up, she would have been much like Grandmother Renfrew – someone who worked hard and cared for her family and knew the joys of nature. And just as her grandmother lived in her heart, so would Emma.

Her thoughts turned then to making her way home. There was no more time to contemplate the past or search the interior of the house for possible hiding places. She'd been gone far too long. Although she was sad to be leaving the family, she felt uplifted that the house would still be part of her life, at least for two more days.

She stepped back and took one more long look at it. The stone house stood majestically overlooking the prairies and Emily felt proud that it was part of her heritage. She touched the stones, seeing in her mind again her great-grandfather and great-uncles working on it. She felt its comfort and such a strong connection that she never wanted to give the house up.

With sudden determination, Emily decided there had to be a way to keep the house. She simply had to get back and deal with it. But thoughts of home made her tremble. She'd have to face her mom. She'd been gone so long that her mom and aunt must be up and searching for her. Not one idea popped into her head as to what to say.

Checking that she had everything she needed, Emily fished the carving out of her pocket and reluctantly bent towards the foundation hole. She took a deep breath, closed her eyes and let it go.

CHAPTER FIFTEEN

A moment later, Emily opened her eyes to bright sunlight and two pairs of eyes staring at her. A groan escaped before she had a chance to stifle it. She had to face them right away.

"Oh, good heavens!" Her mom came to her. "Emily, what's happened to you?"

"You're a mess, kiddo," Aunt Liz said kindly, wrinkling her nose at the pungent odour.

Emily grimaced and scrunched her eyes shut, her mind whirling over how she was going to explain herself this time. Her head ached, and she felt overwrought. The next thing she knew, tears were rolling down her face, but she was smiling, happy to be home and safe. She clung to her mom, wrapping her arms around her. Kate hugged her, and with Aunt Liz on her other side, they walked her into the house. She was limping and her whole body felt like cooked spaghetti.

"I'm okay, Mom," she insisted when they reached the kitchen and tried to deposit her into a chair.

"I think I should call the doctor." Kate looked over at Aunt Liz for confirmation.

"No, Mom! I'll be fine!"

"Can you at least tell us what happened?" her aunt's concerned face hovered near her.

"Give me a few minutes." Emily pointed upstairs. She needed to clean herself up. She couldn't stand the smell of herself and her yucky clothes were beginning to dry onto her skin. A nice long soak in the bathtub seemed like a great idea.

"At least tell us something," her mom said firmly.

"I fell into a slough," Emily shook her head. "I'll explain it all as soon as I clean up."

"I'll get some fresh towels." Aunt Liz bounced up the stairs ahead of her.

Her mom followed behind as Emily limped and groaned with each step. Emily let her mom run the water into the tub, while Aunt Liz poured in some bubble bath crystals. They stood staring at her, until she ordered them to leave. As she undressed, she threw her clothes into the garbage. They were so badly tattered and scorched and stained, she'd never be able to wear them again.

She sank into the warm, bubbly water, letting its healing powers soothe her. She soaked for a long time, then shampooed her hair several times. The water was greyish green when she let it go, so she rinsed herself under a hot shower. The steam helped soothe her sore throat. By the time she was done, almost an hour had passed, and she could hear her mom and aunt discussing her plight outside the door.

"Can we get you anything, Emily?" Aunt Liz asked.

"Do you need any medication or bandages?" Her mom tapped on the door.

"No, I'm fine, Mom," Emily replied, checking herself out in the full-length mirror hung on the door.

Although she had a few sore muscles and a headache, the only other damages were scratches on her arms and legs. She looked much better, except for her singed eyebrows. Wrapping her hair in a towel turban-style and her body in a bathrobe, she stepped out of the bathroom and found herself being examined by her mom and aunt.

"Honestly, I'm okay!" Emily said. "I sure could use something to eat, though."

"Coming right up," said Aunt Liz, giving her a hug.

As she and her mom slowly descended, Emily thought again of how she was going to explain her condition. She decided the truth would be best, but who would believe her? Whatever she came up with, she knew she was facing some serious reprimands, and she'd have to take her medicine in whatever way her mom decided to dole it out. She'd deliberately disobeyed her.

Once settled in a chair at the kitchen table with a

sandwich and a glass of milk in front of her, Emily decided to deal with the situation head-on.

"Mom, Aunt Liz, I've just experienced a prairie fire..."

Before she could go on, Aunt Liz jumped up and rushed to the window. "My heavens, I thought those days were over!"

Her mom dashed for the phone, "Why didn't you say something right away? We'd better call the fire brigade."

"Where is it?" Aunt Liz said, stepping outside to look for smoke in the other directions.

"No, wait, you don't understand," Emily tried to calm them down. "It's not here, well, it is, but just not now. It's in the past."

Emily hadn't planned what to say. She just let the words tumble out, explaining the past few days as best as she could. Her mom and aunt stared at her intently, absorbing everything she said. She felt relieved when she finished. Now she didn't need to sneak around anymore or tell any half-truths.

Suddenly, Kate felt Emily's forehead. She glanced over at Aunt Liz.

"I think she has a fever."

Aunt Liz nodded with a worried look. "You get her tucked into bed, I'll bring the Tylenol."

"Then we'll call the doctor," Kate hustled Emily out of her chair.

"Stop," Emily demanded. "There's nothing wrong with me — well, at least not with the functions of my brain. I can prove that everything happened."

Emily told them about the homestead papers and their mention of the prairie fire.

"That doesn't prove anything," her mom shook her head.

Aunt Liz added, "Except maybe that you are delirious."

"But you saw my clothes. And look at my eyebrows," she pointed to them.

"That doesn't verify what happened to you or where. Maybe you were just over at the neighbours where they're burning stubble," Kate argued.

"That's right. I heard Arnie Kippins talking about doing that yesterday at the auction," Aunt Liz confirmed. "Donald Ferguson got into a heated discussion with him about how it was ruining the environment and not necessary."

"I don't even know where Arnie Kippins lives!" Emily protested.

"Whatever," her mom said, hustling her out of her chair. "Let's get you up to bed for some rest, anyway."

She tried to convince them again. "Remember, when you thought there was a burglar? Well, that was Geordie." She continued to explain.

"We found a bin door had been left open," her mom dismissed her explanation.

"But you must have seen the loose downspout," Emily protested.

"Yes, but that could have happened any time," Aunt Liz answered. "Donald's coming to fix it when he has a chance."

Emily gave up trying to resist the combined force of her mom and aunt. Besides, she was tired and sore. She wasn't sure what parts of her ached from escaping the prairie fire, and what parts were just plain exhaustion.

Once her mom and aunt had her settled in bed in a clean nightgown, Emily pleaded with her mom one more time. "Please, don't call any doctor. I just need to rest."

Her mom conversed quietly with Aunt Liz, and then she responded sternly. "Okay, we'll see how you are a little later and then decide. But if we think it's necessary, we will be calling a doctor."

Emily grimaced, but said no more.

"Have a good rest, kiddo," Aunt Liz said, leaving the room.

Her mom straightened the covers one more time and tucked Grandmother Renfrew's quilt up to Emily's chin, then gave her a light kiss on the forehead.

"Pleasant dreams," she said. Her eyes were full of concern, and Emily thought she detected a few extra worry lines in her face.

"Everything will be fine, Mom," Emily patted her mom's face. "Don't worry."

She closed her eyes and within seconds dozed off. She vaguely heard her mom leave the room and close the door. Then everything went still and black.

When she awoke an hour later, it wasn't because she was fully rested. In fact, her body throbbed all over and she wondered how long it would take to totally recover. Her brain, though, was too active to let her sleep. She had to stop her mom from calling the doctor, and she had to find the box. It might just help her prove that she was telling the truth.

Gingerly, she stepped downstairs and into the living room.

All at once, her mom and Aunt Liz joined her.

"What on earth are you doing now, Emily?" her mom stood with her arms folded over her chest. "You're supposed to be resting."

"I know, Mom, but I had to look for the box." Emily barely acknowledged the pair of them. "Geordie suggested I look at the fireplace again."

At the mention of Geordie, Kate rolled her eyes at Aunt Liz as if to say, "We have a serious problem here." Emily ignored her and knelt at the hearth, where Aunt Liz joined her.

"Let's just go along with this for now," she suggested.

Emily removed the stone and worked the mechanism again. Carefully, she reached inside and did another search of the hidden compartment. In systematic fashion, she tapped and wiggled, and felt around inside.

Exasperated, she rubbed her hands over the sides and the top. Then, near the bottom at the back, she noticed a notch. She clawed at it with her fingernails. All at once, the base of the compartment budged.

"Wow," she said, lifting the bottom board. Underneath was another slender niche. Inside was a small, hand-carved wooden box. She'd found it at last! Emily drew it out to the exclamations of her mom and aunt. It was about fifteen centimetres long, ten centimetres wide, and six centimetres high. A tiny metal clasp held the lid down.

Gently, she caressed the carved flowers and vines on the top as she imagined her great-grandfather cutting carefully into the wood with his chisels. What kind of person was he really? She suddenly wished she'd been able to get to know him. Anyone who could do such intricate work must be patient. He must also have had a great imagination to create the secret compartments.

"Locked, of course!" Kate said, after trying to open it.

"Beautiful carvings, though!" Aunt Liz examined it closer. "Look, Emily. In between the violets: a stylized letter *E*. It's definitely yours."

Emily traced the initial softly. Her great-grandfather had made something special for her. Wait a minute! Something wasn't right here. How could he have made something for her? He didn't even know about her existence. She'd been born long after he'd died. All at once,

Emily knew. This box had belonged to Emma.

Suddenly, Emily realized she didn't have the key with her. What had happened to it? Where had she last had it? She had to find out what was inside!

"I have to find the key!"

Emily dashed upstairs, carrying the box.

CHAPTER SIXTEEN

She rummaged around in her bedroom, checking the nightstand drawer, the pockets in all her discarded clothes. It wasn't anywhere! Stumped, she sat on the edge of the bed and thought about where she'd had it last. Just then her mom and Aunt Liz appeared in her bedroom.

"Don't tell me you've lost the key!" her mom said, looking at her in disbelief.

Emily bit her lip. She tried to think of where it could be. Had she left it in the past?

"Why can't you be more organized, Emily?" her mom asked. "It's not that hard, you know! Just take some time and plan it out. This goes here, that goes there, and then you can always find things."

"I'm sure it's just misplaced temporarily," said Aunt Liz, trying to soften Kate's words.

Emily looked up at her gratefully. Then she faced her mom. Suddenly, everything about her mom seemed clear.

"You know something, Mom? You're right!" Emily stood up.

"What?" Kate asked in disbelief. "I'm right?"

Emily nodded. "Yes. I know I need to be a little more organized, but I'll never be as good at it as you are. I'm just not that kind of person."

She thought of Kate from the past and how her mom was so similar to her. She couldn't seem to stop voicing her opinion. "I know you can't help being the way you are, Mom, any more than I can help the way I am. All right, I can change a little," she admitted. "But what I'm trying to say is that we're all different. I'm not going to let you make me crazy, just because we do things differently. Yes, I've misplaced the key. I'll find it."

She ushered her mom and aunt to the door. "I just need time to figure out where it might be."

Aunt Liz clapped lightly, bowing to Emily, and left. Her mom tried to say something, but Emily held up her hand to stop her.

"Not now, Mom. I need to think!"

She closed the door in her mom's surprised face. When she was sure they were both gone, Emily lay back on her bed and giggled. The tension she felt around her mom seemed to have dissolved. From now on, she was going to have her mom treat her more like an adult, and she was not going to take her mom's bossy ways so seriously.

She had enough to worry about with her parents divorcing, not seeing her dad for a very long time, and trying to save the stone house for the future. Her mind went blank over the lost key, so eventually she gave up and crept downstairs. Maybe if she didn't think about it, she'd remember. She could hear them in the kitchen, their voices muted.

"I don't know what to do about Emily," Kate complained.

"What do you mean?" asked Aunt Liz.

"I just don't understand what's come over her lately. Look at the way she acted upstairs. Ordering me around."

Aunt Liz laughed. "She's growing up. She has her own mind. You should be proud that she's finding out who she is."

"Speaking of her mind, I'm wondering if there isn't something seriously wrong with her. All these stories she's telling."

"I think you have to face it, Kate, your daughter is fey, just like Mom was," Aunt Liz spoke frankly.

"Fey?" Kate questioned.

"Yes, you know, psychic, second sight, woo-woo-WOO-woo."

"I know what it means," Kate replied in disgust. "I just don't believe in it."

"How else are you going to explain what's been happening?"

"Well, she's been seeing ghosts, maybe, but nothing else!" Kate insisted.

"Talking to them too," Aunt Liz said smugly. "And if we were to believe her, interacting with them as well."

Emily burst into the kitchen.

"They're not ghosts," she declared.

"Well, how else do you explain it, then?" her mom demanded.

A sudden smile tugged at the corner of Emily's mouth, when she thought about the similar discussion she'd had with Geordie.

"It's different," she attempted to explain. "I actually went back into pioneer time. Just like I did before, with Emma."

"Oh boy, here we go again." Her mom's look of disbelief, said it all. "Emily, you really have to quit fantasizing."

Emily raised her eyebrows at her mom. "Do you really think that's what I've been doing?"

Kate spluttered, "I have no idea what you've been up to. It all sounds crazy to me!"

"That's just because you don't try to understand it," Emily said. "Don't you believe in ghosts at all? I don't mean the scary haunting kind, but maybe relatives coming back to tell people about something, like they sometimes show on television documentaries."

"There are some amazing stories, all right, but no one can prove they're true," Kate said.

"They can't prove they aren't true, either," Emily grinned.

Aunt Liz gave her the thumbs-up.

"You quit encouraging her!" Kate admonished her sister.

"She made a good point, Kate!" Aunt Liz laughed.

"Fine!" Kate conceded. "I can see I can't win with the two of you. I still don't believe it's true, but you can think what you want."

Kate rose as if to leave the kitchen.

"Wait, Mom," Emily said. "Can we talk about keeping the house?"

Kate's mouth fell open. "You can't be serious!"

"I am serious! I know we need to keep this house in our family. When you know how hard our ancestors worked to build it and keep it, through bad crops and prairie fires, it just doesn't seem right to let it go."

"Look, Gerald Ferguson is going to allow us access to it any time we want," Kate stood with her hands on her hips.

"Yes, but coming to stay in the stone house for a visit isn't the same thing as owning it," Emily argued.

"I'm not even going to discuss it anymore. I know how you feel and I'm sorry. If there was a way to do it, we would have done it by now. End of story." Kate said, leaving the room.

"There has to be a way!" Emily protested.

Aunt Liz looked crestfallen, too. "I'm sorry too, because it's the centre of our family heritage."

Suddenly, Emily's face brightened. "You may just have hit upon something, Aunt Liz!"

"What?" she asked mystified.

"The heritage part." Emily said eagerly.

She began searching through the stack of papers on the end of the counter for the local newspaper she'd been reading, remembering an article about the Wolseley courthouse. At last, she found it, and quickly turned to the right page. She strode over to show her aunt.

"See," she pointed out the article. "It's been declared a heritage site."

Aunt Liz raised her eyebrows. "And so?"

"So, why couldn't we do that with this house?"

"I really doubt it!" said her mom, returning to the room somewhat calmer.

Aunt Liz pondered for a few minutes, scanning the article. "I wonder if this house would meet the criteria for being declared a heritage site?"

"Pfff! What's so special about it?" Kate chided.

"I don't know, but I could phone and find out on Monday," Aunt Liz said. "At least it would be kept from deteriorating."

Aunt Liz looked at Kate. "What do you say, Miss Bossy Boots?" Aunt Liz teased her.

Kate answered slowly. "I suppose it can't hurt to find out."

Emily danced around behind her aunt. "Yes! I knew there had to be something."

"Don't get your hopes up yet," Aunt Liz warned. "There are plenty of stone houses around the area, so it might come to nothing. It doesn't have any particular historical significance."

Aunt Liz held up her hand in anticipation of Emily's protest. "I mean to others besides us!"

"I suppose something that might be in our favour is that we're still living here, and most of the others are abandoned or falling down," her mom said, warming a little to the idea.

"If being a heritage site doesn't work, I've got another idea." Emily grinned at them both. "Why don't we turn the house into a bed and breakfast? We could run it and stay here too." Emily looked excitedly at them both.

"Aunt Liz, you wanted to retire, and a bed and breakfast wouldn't take much work. And Mom, you're always complaining that you'd like to do something different. What could be more perfect?"

Kate groaned. "I don't think so, besides we just had an auction and got rid of everything."

A shadow crossed Emily's face and then she brightened again, and laughed. "I think we still have enough furniture, with all my stuff!" She laughed.

Aunt Liz grinned, "I suppose you're right about that!"

"I'm not saying I'm interested," said Kate, "but there would still be the problem of who owns the place and the upkeep of the grounds."

"You said yourself, Mom, that Gerald doesn't want the house, and he'd have to mow the yard anyway, so what could be so difficult about running the place?"

"I'm sure there are plenty of things!" Kate looked over at Aunt Liz, who had a pensive look on her face.

Emily appealed to her aunt, "We'd just have to cook some meals and do some laundry and a little cleaning. Aunt Liz, you're a whiz at cooking."

Aunt Liz laughed. "You're quite the conniver, Emily!"

"I'll say!" said Kate.

"Have I convinced you yet?" She smiled at her mother.

Kate protested, "No, Em, you haven't. I've got my job to do. How would I ever manage it out here?"

"The Internet!" Emily answered. "Most of what you do, from what I've seen, is all done on your computer anyway."

Kate seemed stumped. "This is all too sudden," she protested. "We'd have a lot of thinking and planning to do before we'd ever consider doing something like that. I doubt it's something we could do full-time."

"But, it's a good idea, isn't it?" Emily asked. "Just let me know what I can do to help!"

"For starters, you can set the table for supper," her mom interjected.

Emily rolled her eyes. "Mom, you are such a damper!"

But Emily smiled, pleased that there might be a chance of keeping the stone house after all.

"You know, Kate," Aunt Liz said as an afterthought. "We could run a bed and breakfast just during the summers."

"Don't you start, too!" Kate moaned.

"I think that's a brilliant idea," Emily said. "Maybe we could even do hiking trails and I could take them on walks."

Aunt Liz laughed. "You are always coming up with a million ideas, Emily. You remind me of our Uncle Geordie."

"What about him?" Emily perked up with interest. She'd forgotten her aunt had known him.

"He was the mad inventor of the family! He was the first in the family to have electricity and running water. He even had an indoor bathroom long before they became fashionable. He built all kinds of contraptions and windmills and electrical things to make his life easier. He drove Aunt Harriett crazy with all his new-fangled gadgets. Sometimes they worked and sometimes they didn't. He was always curious."

Emily laughed, remembering Geordie's interest in the house when he came to visit her.

"Wasn't he instrumental in getting a library set up in the area?" asked Kate.

"Yes, he was. Education became very important to him, and he read so much, learning about the world around him. He had this old set of encyclopedias that he read from cover to cover."

The chatting at suppertime continued to be animated and full of hope for Emily. She could hardly contain herself. Even when she was left alone to do the dishes, while her mom and aunt took their tea onto the veranda to watch the sun setting, she felt happy. Life wasn't so bad after all, except for her parent's divorce. Her father came to mind. A flash of determination came over her and she marched over to the phone.

"Hello, Dad," she said, when she reached him.

"Hi, pumpkin," he answered. "I'm surprised to hear from you. What's up?"

"Dad, before I get into all that, I think I'm getting a little old for that nickname."

"All right, Emily," her dad said. "So, what do you need?"

"I just wondered how your plans were coming for our holiday?"

"I haven't made any arrangements yet. I've been too busy, but I will," he answered. "Why?"

"Well, I miss you and I'm disappointed not to be able see you for such a long time. And I was wondering if you really want to see me?"

"Of course I do," he sputtered.

"It doesn't seem like it." Emily could feel the hurt and anger rising within. She said, "Face it, Dad. You don't want me around. "

"Emily, that's not true!" he declared. "Where did you get that idea from?"

"Well, you sure aren't making much of an effort to see me soon, are you?"

"I thought I'd explained the situation and you understood," he said.

"Well, I don't. That's way too long to wait," she answered. "I have to go."

"Wait, Emily, don't hang up," he pleaded. "We should talk about this."

"Some other time, maybe. I can't right now," she said. "I'm going to hang up." She let the receiver drop into the cradle and leaned against the wall, weak with emotion. She took a couple of deep breaths and thought about what she'd just done. At least, she'd told him how she felt. With a wry smile, she realized how her mother must have felt when her dad explained why he couldn't be home, all those times. His reasons must have felt like excuses, as if he didn't want to try very hard to spend time with them.

Suddenly, she heard a male voice outside. As she quickly wiped the dampness out of her eyes, she strained to make out who it was. She heard her mom and aunt laugh and then the voice again. It was Donald. She heard the voices move away from the door and then some hammering against the house. He must be fixing the clamps on the downspout. He sure showed up often these days.

A little twinge of jealousy touched her and then was gone. Donald was a nice man, and Emily was confident her mom wouldn't do anything so rash as to bring him into their lives any time soon. He was a good friend to them all, though, and they were fortunate to have him around to help. Especially if they were going to open a bed and breakfast! Emily smiled at the thought, and was just about to join them outside, when she suddenly remembered the key. Where had she left it?

As she headed upstairs again and made a pit stop in the bathroom, an idea struck her. She dove over to the garbage can in the corner. She lifted the dripping mass of bedraggled clothes from it and felt in her pants pocket. There it was! She hadn't remembered putting it there. Nevertheless, she rinsed it off, and leapt up the stairs to her room, taking them two at a time. Eagerly, she inserted the key into the lock. Yes! It fit!

Emily hesitated before opening the carved box. Should she call her mom and aunt first? Would they be disappointed if she didn't wait? She heard their voices down below. They must have come into the house again. Donald must have left. Perhaps she'd just take a little peek. Flipping up the clasp, she edged the lid open.

A small hand mirror, beautifully carved with inlaid stones in the handle, nestled in blue satin. It looked Old World to her, as if it belonged to some ancient time. She didn't know the names of all the stones, but she did recognize garnets and topaz. She had the same stones in some of her jewellery, which her dad had given her as gifts when he returned from his various trips. Shutting the lid gently, she carried it downstairs.

When she found her mom and aunt, they were sitting in the living room, trying to find a decent show on the television set. They took one look at her face and what she held in her hands and they turned it off. Emily presented the box to them, opening the lid carefully.

"Wow," Aunt Liz stared in awe at the striking stones embedded on the back of the mirror.

"It's beautiful," said her mom. "But this doesn't look like something your great-grandfather would be passing on to you."

"It looks way older than something he would have bought, too," agreed Aunt Liz.

"That's because it wasn't meant for me," Emily said.

"Well, I know it's not mine, either," said Aunt Liz.

"No, it's not. I'm sure it belonged to Emma."

Aunt Liz and Kate were speechless.

Emily drew it out of the box and turned it over in her hands. She felt a current of power and connection running through her. As she held it, she saw Emma's face in the mirror, and beside her, she could see Gran Renfrew, and they were both smiling. Emily could also see other women from times gone by, and sensed a feeling of bonding warmth and goodness.

"I don't know that it was ever meant to be found," she said.

"Just by the very fact that you have it in your hands, I think it was," said Aunt Liz. "And by you."

Her mom seemed subdued and when she spoke, she said, "Yes, I agree. I know your gran would have wanted you to have it."

"I wonder what its history is?" Emily said.

"No doubt, it's a Scottish relic, or at least of Celtic origin, but there's no telling how old it is. Although I'd venture to say it dates back to very early times," Aunt Liz guessed.

"Well, however old it is, I will treasure it." Emily gently laid it back in the box.

The phone rang then, and when Aunt Liz answered, she passed it over to Emily.

"Hi, Emily," her dad said from the other end of the line.

"Hi, Dad," Emily replied, her fingers trembling slightly. What was he going to tell her now? That he didn't want to see her at all? Was he angry? She felt her throat tighten.

"Em, I was just wondering, do you have any plans for the next couple of weeks?" he asked, sounding optimistic.

"Not really," she answered, as calmly as she could. "Just hanging out with my friends, going to the pool and the mall. That kind of stuff."

"Would you consider coming on a little research expedition with me to Scotland? I'll have to work some, but I thought you might like it in the highlands. We'll have a cottage to stay in, and there are horses and trail rides, and castles to explore and..."

"Dad, Dad!" she cut into his description. "It doesn't matter what it has. I'd love to come."

"You would?"

"Yes!" Emily was at a loss for words. Her dad wanted to see her, right away.

"Can I speak to your mom, then, and we'll make your flight arrangements?"

"Sure, Dad. Thanks. See you soon." She handed the phone to her mom.

Emily took the mirror out of the box and studied her face. Her eyes shone with delight. There were so many things to be happy about; she didn't know where to begin to count them.

No, her parents weren't getting back together again, and no, she probably wasn't going to travel back in time again to see Geordie and the rest of the Elliott family, and no, she knew the days ahead with her mom wouldn't always be smooth sailing, but for all of that, she was content with her life. There were many possibilities, and she felt certain that somehow they'd figure out how to keep Grandmother Renfrew's house.

She could appreciate the hard work and the way of life of her ancestors more because she'd experienced some of it, but she didn't want to live that way. The modern conveniences, indoor plumbing, going to the movies, and travelling with her dad from time to time, would be just fine.

When her mom replaced the receiver, Emily went over to hug her. Surprised, her mom wrapped her arms around her. Emily said, "I'm so glad we live here, in this time, right here, right now."

SCOTTISH VOCABULARY

bairn - *a child*

cannae - *cannot*

feart - *scared*

hen - *term of endearment*

lass - *a girl, a young woman*

lassie - *a young lass, a term of endearment*

kirk - *church*

wee - *little, young*

Geordie - *short for George - pronounced jor'-dee*

SCOTCH OATCAKES

1 cup flour
1/2 tsp salt
1/4 tsp baking soda
2 cups rolled oats
1/2 cup shortening
1/2 cup cold water

Sift flour, soda, and salt into a mixing bowl. Add rolled oats and mix well. Rub in shortening, add cold water, roll thin. Cook on top of the stove or griddle. They can also be baked on a cookie sheet in the oven at 350°F until they are lightly browned.

BIBLIOGRAPHY

Holt, Faye Reineberg, *Out of the Flames: Fires and Fire Fighting on the Canadian Prairies,* Fifth House Ltd., Calgary, AB, 1998.

Long, Charles, *The Stonebuilder's Primer,* Firefly Books Ltd., 1988.

Parley, Kay, "Remember Assiniboia," *The Wolseley Bulletin,* Friday, February 18th, 2005.

Parley, Kay, *They Cast a Long Shadow: The Story of Moffat, Saskatchewan,* Desktop Publishing by Root Woman & Dave ™, Saskatoon, 1965.

ACKNOWLEDGEMENTS

Thank you to Kay Parley for her assistance in my "getting things right" with the Moffat area and the people who settled there and for forgiving the liberty I have taken in skewing the time somewhat to make my story work. Thank you for the wonderful material in your book, *They Cast a Long Shadow: The Story of Moffat, Saskatchewan,* which I used extensively to ensure that my facts were accurate. Any errors are my own.

The actual Moffat area was settled much earlier than when my characters came to Canada and I have therefore set my story on the nearby eastern fringes of the Moffat community, in what was settled later as the Glenavon area. The settlers from Glenavon identified with Moffat, associated themselves closely with the people of Moffat, and were often related to them.

I am proud to be associated with the Moffat and Glenavon communities, and to have spent several early years living there. I appreciate the many stories my relatives shared about our pioneering families. I really did have a great-uncle Geordie, just like Emily.

Thank you to my son, Aaron, for his patience, assistance, and support, which is encouraging and reinforcing.

I wish to express my sincere gratitude to my editor, Barbara Sapergia, whose gentle steering and thoughtful resourcefulness brought so much to this book.

As always, I appreciate the valuable team at Coteau Books: Nik, Karen, Duncan, Joanne, Deborah, and Melanie for their excellent attention to detail, resourceful promotion, creativity, and continued support.

ABOUT THE AUTHOR

JUDITH SILVERTHORNE is the author of five previous books, including the prequel to this one, *The Secret of Sentinel Rock*, which received the Saskatchewan Book Award for Children's Literature in 1996. The books in her Dinosaur series, *Dinosaur Hideout* and *Dinosaur Breakout*, have also been listed for several awards.

Judith Silverthorne works as a writer, film producer, and cultural administrator in Regina. For more information on Judith and her work, consult her Web site at: *www.judithsilverthorne.ca*.

FROM MANY PEOPLES

Coteau Books began to develop the *From Many Peoples* series of novels for young readers over a year ago, as a celebration of Saskatchewan's Centennial. We looked for stories that would illuminate life in the province from the viewpoints of young people from different cultural groups and we're delighted with the stories we found.

We're especially happy with the unique partnership we have been able to form with the LaVonne Black Memorial Fund in support of *From Many Peoples*. The Fund was looking for projects it could support to honour a woman who had a strong interest in children and their education, and decided that the series was a good choice. With their help, we are able to provide free books to every school in the province, tour the authors across the province, and develop additional materials to support schools in using *From Many Peoples* titles.

This partnership will bring terrific stories to young readers all over Saskatchewan, honour LaVonne Black and her dedication to the children of this province, and help us celebrate Saskatchewan's Centennial. Thank you to everyone involved.

Nik Burton
Managing Editor, Coteau Books

LAVONNE BLACK

My sister LaVonne was born in Oxbow, Saskatchewan, and grew up on a small ranch near North-
gate. She spent a lot of time riding horses and always had
a dog or a cat in her life. LaVonne's favourite holiday
was Christmas. She loved to sing carols and spoil children with gifts. People were of genuine interest to her.
She didn't care what you did for a living, or how much
money you made. What she did care about was learning
as much about you as she could in the time she had with
you.

We are proud of our LaVonne, a farm girl who
started school in a one-room schoolhouse and later presented a case to the Supreme Court of Canada. Her
work took her all over Saskatchewan, and she once said

that she didn't know why some people felt they had to go other places, because there is so much beauty here. LaVonne's love and wisdom will always be with me. She taught me that what you give of yourself will be returned to you, and that you should love, play, and live with all your heart.

LaVonne felt very strongly about reading and education, and the LaVonne Black Memorial Fund and her family hope that you enjoy this series of books.

Trevor L. Black, little brother
Chair, LaVonne Black Memorial Fund

LAVONNE BLACK was a tireless advocate for children in her years with the Saskatchewan School Boards Association. Her dedication, passion, and commitment were best summed up in a letter she wrote to boards of education one month before her death, when she announced her decision to retire:

"I thank the Association for providing me with twenty-three years of work and people that I loved. I was blessed to have all that amid an organization with a mission and values in which I believed. School trustees and the administrators who work for them are special people in their commitment, their integrity, and their caring. I was truly blessed and am extremely grateful for the opportunities and experiences I was given."

LaVonne was killed in a car accident on July 19, 2003. She is survived by her daughter, Jasmine, and her fiancé, Richard. We want so much to thank her for all she gave us. Our support for this book series, *From Many Peoples,* is one way to do this. Thank you to everyone who has donated to her Memorial Fund and made this project possible.

Executive, Staff, and member boards of
The Saskatchewan School Boards Association

Also

FROM MANY PEOPLES

CHRISTMAS AT WAPOS BAY

by Jordan Wheeler & Dennis Jackson

At Christmas time in Northern Saskatch-ewan, three Cree children –
Talon, Raven, and T-Bear – visit their *Moshum's* (Grandfather's) cabin to
learn about traditional ways and experience a life-changing adventure.

ISBN: 978-1-55050-324-1 – $8.95

NETTIE'S JOURNEY

Nettie'   her
grandd   WWI
to the   it

ADELINE'S DREAM

by Linda Aksomitis

Adeline has to struggle to make a place for herself when she comes to
Canada from Germany. Life in her new home is definitely dramatic, but by
Christmas time she starts to feel a sense of belonging in her new home.

ISBN: 978-1-55050-323-4 – $8.95

Available at fine bookstores everywhere.

COTEAU
BOOKS
FOR KIDS

Amazing Stories. Amazing Kids.

WWW.COTEAUBOOKS.COM